She shook
"I don't beli

D0628440

"Would a form
feel better, Miss Nichols?" he asked."

"I know this must seem very funny to you," Danielle said coldly, "but I'm not in the habit of going off with strangers."

"You're right," he said solemnly. "Two people who are about to set off on a journey together should at least know each other's name." He made a sweeping bow. "Lee Bradford at your service, mam'selle."

"Am I supposed to know your name, or something?"

"You've never seen me in ads for the racetrack?"

Danielle looked blank. "You can't be a jockey. They're short, aren't they?"

He reached up slowly and pulled off her glasses. There was laughter in his eyes again. "Cars," he said softly. "Race cars. I'm a driver, Miss Nichols."

SANDRA MARTON says she has always believed in the magic of storytelling and the joy of living happily ever after with that special someone. She wrote her first romance story when she was nine and fell madly in love at the age of sixteen with the man she would eventually marry. Today, after raising two sons and an assortment of four-legged creatures, Sandra and her husband live in a house on a hilltop in a quiet corner of Connecticut.

Books by Sandra Marton

HARLEQUIN PRESENTS

1194—DEAL WITH THE DEVIL
1219—CHERISH THE FLAME
1244—EYE OF THE STORM
1277—FLY LIKE AN EAGLE
1308—FROM THIS DAY FORWARD
1347—NIGHT FIRES
1379—CONSENTING ADULTS

Don't miss any of our special offers. Write to us at the following address for information on our newest releases.

Harlequin Reader Service
P.O. Box 1397, Buffalo, NY 14240
Canadian address: P.O. Box 603,
Fort Erie, Ont. L2A 5X3

SANDRA MARTON

garden of eden

Harlequin Books

TORONTO • NEW YORK • LONDON
AMSTERDAM • PARIS • SYDNEY • HAMBURG
STOCKHOLM • ATHENS • TOKYO • MILAN

Harlequin Presents first edition November 1991
ISBN 0-373-11411-7

Original hardcover edition published in 1990
by Mills & Boon Limited

GARDEN OF EDEN

Copyright © 1990 by Sandra Marton. All rights reserved.
Except for use in any review, the reproduction or utilization
of this work in whole or in part in any form by any electronic,
mechanical or other means, now known or hereafter invented,
including xerography, photocopying and recording,
or in any information storage or retrieval system, is forbidden without
the permission of the publisher, Harlequin Enterprises Limited,
225 Duncan Mill Road, Don Mills, Ontario, Canada M3B 3K9.

All the characters in this book have no existence outside the
imagination of the author and have no relation whatsoever to
anyone bearing the same name or names. They are not even
distantly inspired by any individual known or unknown to the
author, and all incidents are pure invention.

® are Trademarks registered in the United States Patent and
Trademark Office and in other countries.

Printed in U.S.A.

CHAPTER ONE

DANIELLE wondered if the man was watching her. She had the feeling he had been, ever since he'd entered the first-class lounge. She'd been alone and, when the door had swung open, it had been natural to glance up from her book and look at the new arrival. Having company had seemed a welcome prospect.

But she hadn't expected anyone like him. Tall, broad-shouldered, he had the kind of rugged good looks that Danielle had only before seen on the movie screen. He looked nothing like the weary, middle-aged businessmen travelling on expense accounts her friend Ginny had sworn were the only people who used the airlines' private lounges between flights.

'Look,' Ginny had said patiently, 'you have a two-hour lay-over between planes. Why should you sit in a noisy terminal all that time while some guy who sells widgets relaxes in style? I have a friend who's a flight attendant. He can get you into the VIP lounge.'

Danielle had protested, saying that her discount ticket on Air France hardly entitled her to such perks. She would feel out of place, she'd told Ginny. But her friend had been determined.

'Jack says it's no problem. And you'll probably be all by yourself anyway. After a while, you'll be dying for company.'

Ginny had been right. The lounge had turned out to be big, handsomely furnished—and as impersonal as a dental surgery. Danielle drank more coffee than was good for her, read a glossy fashion magazine until her eyes felt glazed, and kept glancing at her watch, as if she could somehow will the time to move faster. But she never did resolve the feeling of being out of place.

That was why she felt so uncomfortable now.

Her first thought, when she'd seen the man, had been that he belonged here and she didn't. And then something had happened, something she still couldn't understand.

His eyes—so blue they were almost violet—had met hers. Suddenly, the room had seemed to shimmer with electricity. Danielle had heard the racing beat of her own heart, and then the man had smiled, a private little tilt of his finely sculpted mouth that had sent colour flooding into her face.

Danielle had wrenched her head away, forcing herself to stare blindly out of the window, and finally she'd heard the soft sound of footfalls as he'd crossed the room and then the soft shift of leather as he'd settled into a chair.

Silence had fallen around her again and the moments had dragged by while she'd tried to decide what to do next. Her impulse had been to bolt out of the door to the public lounge. But that was silly. There was no reason to run—it was just that, every few minutes, she felt the nape of her neck tingle with the awareness of his eyes, felt her blood surge wildly beneath her skin. And then her pulse would begin to quicken until it drummed so loudly she was certain he could hear it.

All of which was, of course, ridiculous. It was just her imagination—there was no reason to think he was looking at her. He was probably reading a newspaper or dozing or——

'Excuse me.' She looked up, startled. The man was standing beside her, holding a newspaper in his hand and smiling. 'I was wondering—do you have the correct time? My watch seems to have stopped.'

'It's five past seven,' Danielle said, looking pointedly from him to the large clock on the wall.

His eyes followed hers and his smile broadened. 'Now, how could I have missed seeing that?' She said nothing, and he put his hand on the chair beside hers. 'May I?'

She caught her bottom lip between her teeth. 'If you like.'

Their eyes met as he sat down and she looked away quickly, bending her head over the book in her lap, staring at it, willing herself to read it. But the print blurred before her eyes. She heard the rustle of paper. Out of the corner of her eye, she could see that he was absorbed in the news.

Danielle stared at the book again, trying to get the jumbled letters to make sense. What on earth was the matter with her? The man seated next to her was good-looking, yes. But she'd seen good-looking men before. And he was flirting—she was certain of it. Well, so what? Men had flirted with her before. Sometimes, it was even fun to flirt back. Just a little, of course: a smile, perhaps even a brief conversation, and then you both went on your way.

But there was something different about this man. He was nothing like the men she knew back home. He was more worldly, she could see that at a glance. And then there was the way he looked, that taut body and hard, handsome face and——

'Are you taking the non-stop to Nice?'

She looked up. He was smiling politely, and his words were polite, too. But there was something else in those blue eyes, something that made her breath catch. Danielle touched her tongue to her lips which felt, suddenly, as dry as the desert.

'Yes,' she said.

He nodded. 'Me, too. Are you on vacation?'

'Yes.' Was this one stilted word all she could manage?

'Have you been to the Riviera before?' She shook her head and he smiled. 'You'll love it. It's crowded this time of year, but there are some out of the way spots the tourists haven't found yet.' His eyes swept over her face. 'Where are you staying? Perhaps we could——'

'No,' she said quickly. His eyebrows rose and, to her horror, she felt a blush spread across her cheeks. 'I mean, I'm not really on vacation. I—I've promised to do some work while I'm away, and. . .'

Oh, God! He was laughing at her. Well, why wouldn't he? She was making a fool of herself, dammit—or *he* was. Yes, that was it. He knew he was making her uneasy and it amused him.

Enough is enough, she thought, drawing herself up, and from some inner reserve she dredged up a cool smile. 'Excuse me,' she said politely, 'but I'd like to finish my book.'

She looked down at the book as if she were about to do just that. She couldn't read a word, of course, she was too frazzled. But at least she'd managed to silence him. . .

He laughed softly. 'Can you really do that before our flight is called?'

Danielle blinked, then stared at the book in her lap. She had it open to the first chapter, but the book was easily three hundred pages long.

Heat rushed to her face again. OK, she thought, OK, that was it. There was another half-hour to go before boarding, and she wasn't going to sit here and provide sport for some jaded jet-setter.

She looked away from that smug twinkle in his eyes and slipped her shoulder-bag over her arm. Carefully, she tucked her book into the pocket of her carry-on, then rose from her chair. All she had to do was walk across the lounge, and——

'Miss?'

She jumped as his hand fell lightly on her shoulder. How had he moved so quickly? And so silently. But here he was, standing beside her. He was still smiling, but now it was slow and sexy and very, very knowing.

'I didn't mean to startle you. But I thought——'

'You thought wrong,' she said. Her voice was cold, despite the sudden race of her heart. 'Now, if you'd step aside. . .'

His smile became a grin. 'No problem,' he said easily. 'Except that you'll have a tough time getting on the plane without this.'

Danielle stared at his outstretched hand. 'What is. . .?'

'I think it's your boarding pass.' He laughed at the look on her face. 'Go on, look at it and see for yourself.'

She hesitated, then took the envelope from him and peered at it. He was right, it *was* her boarding pass. But how——?

He smiled. 'You dropped it when you stood up,' he said, as if he'd read her thoughts.

Danielle swallowed. 'I didn't. . .' Their eyes met, and she swallowed again. 'Thank you,' she said stiffly.

'Thank you? Is that all you can manage after what I've done?'

She stared at him. 'What—what do you mean?'

He smiled again. 'I won't feel thanked until you have a drink with me.'

'No,' she said. 'I—I can't. My flight——'

'Our flight won't be boarding for another half-hour. We've plenty of time.'

She shook her head. 'Thanks for the offer, but——'

'Coffee, then. Or tea.'

'No. No, I—I don't want anything, thank you. I just. . .' This was ridiculous, she thought. He'd reduced her to sounding like an idiot. 'Goodbye,' she said, and before he could answer she hurried past him, pushed open the door, and stepped into the corridor.

She let out her breath as the door swung safely shut behind her. Her knees felt like jelly, and she sagged back against the wall. What a stellar performance that had been! She'd acted like a schoolgirl. No, not even that. The giggling teenage girls in her senior French class would have handled themselves better than she'd just done.

With a sigh, she gathered up her things and made her way through the terminal to the public lounge. She'd felt out of place in the VIP lounge, that was the trouble. The stranger had belonged there, not she. This wasn't a good beginning, she thought glumly. If she felt out of place now, what was going to happen when she got to France? Here she was, off to spend the summer with a bunch of people she had about as much in common with as—as she had with that man.

God. It was going to be a disaster.

There was a vacant seat at the far end of the lounge, and she sank into it and put her carry-on at her feet. 'Be sure and send me a postcard the minute you get to Nice,' Ginny had said, but why wait that long? She could compose the card in her head this very minute.

Dear Ginny, I'd like to strangle you for talking me into this.

Danielle sighed wearily. Be honest, she told herself, it wasn't Ginny's doing any more than it was anyone else's—except her own. Oh, she'd protested a lot. But the truth was that her fate had been sealed five days before, when Val had first telephoned. Her cousin's offer had just been too hard to resist.

The phone had rung in the middle of the night, awakening Danielle from deep sleep. The test papers she'd marked and left on her night table had slid to the floor as she groped groggily for the instrument. When she'd finally found it and brought it to her ear, the tinny voice on the line was almost drowned out by the heavy crackle of static.

'Hello?' she said hoarsely. 'Hello? Who is this?'

'Danni? It's me, Val. Can you hear me?'

Danielle sat up quickly, as wide awake as if she'd been doused with cold water. She switched on the lamp and stared at her bedside clock. Five a.m., she thought, and her stomach knotted with alarm.

'What's wrong, Val? Has Aunt Helen had another attack? Did Uncle John——?'

Impatience coloured her cousin's voice. 'For goodness' sake, Danni, don't be so melodramatic. Mom's fine. Does something have to be wrong for me to call you?'

Danielle sank back against the pillows. 'It's five in the morning,' she answered. 'The last time I heard from you was—what? Four months ago? Six? You sent me a card from Majorca, I think it was.' Her voice grew dry. 'You can hardly blame me for being a little surprised.'

'I just wanted to say hi, Danni. I guess I forgot about the time difference, though.' Val's voice grew silky. 'I think of you a lot, even if sometimes I do forget to call. Aren't you my favourite cousin?'

Danielle sighed. 'Val. . .'

'You are, aren't you? My favourite cousin?'

It was impossible not to smile. 'I'm not just your favourite cousin, I'm your *only* cousin,' Danielle said, falling easily into the old childhood routine.

Both women laughed and suddenly the static faded, as if their shared laughter had cleared the air.

'How have you been, Danni?'

'Fine. How about you?'

'Oh, I'm terrific. Busy, too. I've been everywhere the past few months, did Mom tell you?'

'Mmm. I spoke with Aunt Helen a couple of weeks ago. She said you'd been to Rome and to London on modelling assignments.' Danielle smiled as she pushed the tumble of light brown curls from her face. 'Lucky you.'

'Lucky me is right. Just wait until you hear where I am now.'

'Yes, you said something about a time difference. Are you in Europe?'

Valerie laughed softly. 'Mom says you're still teaching French at Taft High. Is she right?'

'What else would I be doing? But what does that have to do with——?'

'Where's the one place on earth you'd rather be than anywhere else, French teacher?'

Danielle's eyes widened. 'You mean—Val, are you really in France?'

'That's where I am, all right. I'm on the Côte d'Azur, in a little town just outside Nice. Are you green with envy?'

'I will be if you tell me you're there on vacation,' Danielle said, sighing. 'At least tell me you're working hard—if that's what you can call it when you model gorgeous clothes for a famous *couturier*.'

Her cousin laughed. 'Didn't Mom tell you? I'm not modelling any more. Somehow, they just got around to realising I'm only five feet eight.' She paused. 'I'm here with a film company.'

Danielle sat up and switched the phone to her other ear. 'A film company? Don't tell me you finally landed an acting role, Val! Oh, I'm so happy for you. I know how hard you——'

'I'm not exactly *in* the film, Danni.'

Danielle frowned. 'What kind of job do you have, then?'

'Well, see, I heard about this film Barney Wexler was casting, and I thought I'd have a go at it. I'd met Barney a few years ago, when I was doing a charity fashion show in LA, and ——'

'I thought you just said you weren't in the film.'

'I'm not.' Valerie's voice dropped to a conspiratorial

whisper, just as it had when they were children. 'But I've got my foot in the door. I wangled a job as Barney's secretary.'

The thought of Valerie, who didn't know a typewriter from a typesetter, working as secretary to a film producer made Danielle laugh aloud. 'Come on, Val, don't try to kid me. I know better.'

Valerie hesitated. 'Well, actually, Barney didn't hire me to do a whole lot of secretarial stuff. I'm more of an administrative assistant. You know, I set up his appointments, arrange his day. . .' She hesitated. 'And I guess you could say I'm his liaison to the French-speaking crew members.'

Danielle blinked. The only thing more outlandish than imagining her cousin as a secretary was imagining her as an interpreter. 'His what?' she said slowly.

'His liaison. Well, only in day-to-day stuff on the set. I type up notices and post them, that kind of thing. Barney has a French guy for all the rest, to deal with the officials and the townspeople and. . .'

It was hard to know whether to laugh or cry. 'But you don't speak French,' Danielle said gently.

'I studied it, the same as you,' Valerie said defensively. 'Well, you were better at it than I was, sure, but. . .'

Danielle shook her head. Amazing, she thought. Val hadn't changed a bit over the years. When they'd been teenagers, she'd managed to talk her way into and out of almost everything. It was how she'd got Danielle to do most of her homework and chores.

But this little escapade took the cake. Val, acting as liaison to French-speaking crew members on a film set? It was impossible. It was——

'. . . as good as you ever were, Danielle. Right?'

Danielle cleared her throat. 'I'm sorry, Val. Did you ask me something?'

'I asked if you still spoke French as well as you always did. But you must, if you're teaching it.'

'I suppose. But what——?'

Her cousin let out her breath. 'Do you know, we've been on location almost a week now,' she said. 'And I just keep thinking about you, and how much you'd love this place.'

Danielle sighed. 'You're right. I told you, I'm green with envy. What's the name of the town you're staying in?'

'Ste Agathe. It's in the mountains.'

Danielle closed her eyes, visualising the rocky escarpments rising behind the little villages that dotted the golden Mediterranean coast. 'It must be lovely,' she said softly. 'I wish I could——'

'You can,' Val said quickly. 'That's why I called. I want you to come and spend your summer vacation with me.'

Danielle sat bolt upright. 'What did you say?'

'I said I'd like you to vacation here, in Ste Agathe. Won't that be terrific?'

The offer stunned her. No word from Valerie for months, and now, suddenly. . .

'Danielle? Do I have my timing right? School's almost out, isn't it?'

Danielle touched her tongue to her lips. 'Yes. It ends Friday. But——'

'Please, say you'll do it.' Valerie's voice rose with excitement. 'Just think—you can see the Côte d'Azur and the Riviera, you could even go to Paris for a couple of days, and it won't cost you a penny.' She laughed. 'Well, not much more than a penny. You'd have to foot the side-trips and your fare. But the rest would be free. You'd have an all-expenses-paid summer here.'

Danielle laughed shakily. 'Val, listen, I can't just——'

'The company's put us all up—I have two rooms in a beautiful old *auberge*, it's more than big enough for the both of us. And I can't even put a dent in my per diem meal allowance. Come on, Danielle, say you'll do it. We'll have such fun together—it'll be like old times.'

Like old times. Danielle's cramped bedroom seemed to shimmer in the pre-dawn greyness. For a moment, the pine-panelled walls glowed with a pale pink light, the dark furniture turned gold and white, and the room was transformed into the one she'd shared with Valerie after Aunt Helen and Uncle John had taken her in following the deaths of both her parents in less than a year.

'You girls are sisters now,' Aunt Helen had said, clasping their hands together. 'Won't that be lovely?'

But they'd barely been friends. Not that Danielle hadn't tried. Always a shy child, she had been devastated by the sudden loss of her parents, and she'd longed to get close to her beautiful cousin. But they had been worlds apart. At twelve, Val had been caught up with boys and clothes and make-up; Danielle had been too shy for boys and too plain to worry about make-up and clothes. In fact, the only thing they'd really had in common, aside from their shared bedroom, had been their classes and their chores, and eventually it had been Danielle who'd borne the responsibility for most of those.

'Danielle? Danielle—for goodness' sake, have we got a bad connection or something? I can't hear you at all.'

Danielle blinked and swung her legs to the floor. 'Thanks for asking me, Val,' she said slowly. 'But I really don't think——'

'Come on, say you'll come.' Val's voice grew soft. 'Aren't you my favourite cousin?'

'I'm not just your favourite cousin,' Danielle answered automatically, 'I'm your *only*——'

That's right. You are. And it's time we spent some time together, the way we used to.'

Danielle drew a breath. 'Val?' she said slowly. 'Is there some kind of problem there? I mean, is something wrong?'

'For heaven's sake, nothing's wrong. Haven't I already said that? Mother is fine. Her latest tests were all negative. Daddy's fine, too. I just called because you're my favourite——'

'Come on, Val. What is it?'

There was a brief silence, and then the whisper of Val's transatlantic sigh. 'There *is* a little favour you could do for me if you came for a visit. You see, somehow or other, Barney—Mr Wexler, my boss?—well, somehow he got the idea I speak French better than I really can. I mean, he deals with a lot of French people here.'

'I thought you said all you had to do was post notices.'

'Well, that's what I thought. But other things keep cropping up, and Barney's interpreter isn't always here. Sometimes he's in Nice on business, or——'

'Did you tell this Mr Wexler you were fluent in the language?'

There was another silence. 'No,' Val said finally, 'not exactly. I just told him the truth, that I'd done very well in my French classes.'

Despite herself, Danielle began to laugh. 'Val,' she said patiently, '*I* did very well, remember? You used to copy my homework. And I drilled you like crazy before each exam.'

'And you could do that now,' Val said eagerly. 'Well, not drill me, but you could help me deal with some of the office work. And you could field some of the calls that come in—honestly, French people talk a hundred miles an hour. It's so hard to understand a word they say.' Her voice softened. 'Mom thinks it's a terrific idea.'

'You already spoke to Aunt Helen about this? But——'

'She says you could use a change of scene. She says the accident upset you a lot.' There was a brief silence. 'I really meant to call you, Danni. Was it very awful?'

Danielle closed her eyes. 'Yes,' she whispered finally. 'It was terrible.'

'What was his name? Teddy?'

'Eddie. Eddie Chancellor. You knew him, Val. He was two years ahead of us in school.'

'Was he on the football team or anything?'

Danielle smiled at the thought. 'No. He was on the debating team.'

'I wouldn't remember him, then.' For a moment, the offhand carelessness of the remark angered Danielle, but then Valerie sighed and her voice filled with concern. 'I'm really sorry,' she said. 'When did it happen?'

'Eight months. It's been eight months since——'

'Getting away would be good for you. And you'd save my life. Really.'

Danielle smiled again. 'You always were too dramatic.'

'Well, it's true.' Valerie's voice grew soft. 'I really need you here.' There was a sudden crackle of static. 'Listen, I have to get off the phone now. I'll send you the directions to Ste Agathe, OK? You won't have any trouble finding it. There's this road that goes straight from Nice into the mountains——'

'I haven't said I'm coming,' Danielle said quickly.

'Of course you're coming.' Static crackled again, and then Danielle thought she heard the distant sound of a man's deep voice, followed by husky laughter. She hunched over the phone, straining to hear.

'Val? Are you still there?'

'I'm here,' Val said in a sort of breathless whisper,

and then she laughed softly. 'In a minute. Yes. Well, I'm asking her now.'

'Who are you talking to?'

'Danielle, listen, I really have to run. You just make your flight reservations. Do you have a passport? And you'll need a visa. Oh, and I guess you'll need a rental car to get here from the airport. And——'

'What's your number there? How can I reach you? Val?'

The phone went dead. Danielle hung up slowly, then leaned back against the pillows and tried to imagine Val as an administrative assistant on a film set. The locale sounded glamorous enough, but the job sounded stodgy—nothing like the things her cousin had tried so far: modelling, commercials, even summer theatre once. Val had always been beautiful, and she'd gone easily from high school graduation into a world where that beauty, rather than the ability to conjugate verbs or add a column of figures, had been all she needed to succeed. An administrative assistant, Danielle thought again. Well, that only proved how out of touch they were.

She yawned, got to her feet, then walked to the window and opened the curtains. The June morning was painting the sky with gold. The day was already warm, and the air smelled faintly of the cornfields that stretched away to the Missouri horizon.

Lazily, Danielle stretched her arms high over her head. She was tired, but there was no sense in trying to go back to sleep now. She'd shower, dress, have her breakfast—and think about Val's invitation.

A whole summer in France, she thought as she pulled off her nightshirt and dropped it on the bed. What a vacation that would be! She'd never really done any travelling, except for last winter's trip to visit Aunt Helen and Uncle John in their new retirement home in Arizona.

And Val was right—she really could do with a change. The winter had been long and harsh. And the accident had taken a terrible toll. She still had visions of Eddie lying in the road, his blood turning the rain-slicked tarmac red as his life had drained away.

Danielle shook her head and marched to the bathroom. No. She wouldn't think about that awful day any more. Quickly, she stepped into the bath and turned on the shower. Brooding about Eddie wouldn't bring him back. And, now that she thought about it, a trip to Europe wouldn't do it, either. What it *would* do was exhaust her bank account—room and board might be free, but the fare wasn't.

The more she thought, the more negatives there were. Val might be comfortable on a glitzy film set, but would she? And then there was Val herself—could they even get on together for a whole summer? They'd been dissimilar enough when they were teenagers; what did they have in common now?

Danielle lathered a face-cloth and began scrubbing herself. She'd call Aunt Helen this evening and get Val's phone number, and then she'd call her cousin and tell her thanks, but no thanks. And that would be the end of that.

But it hadn't been. 'Are you nuts?' Ginny had demanded when she mentioned Val's invitation in the faculty-room at lunch. 'A free trip to France, and you're turning it down?'

It had been useless to keep repeating that the trip wasn't free. It was *almost* free, her friend had insisted. And not even an explanation of why Val had really tendered the invitation was enough to dim her friend's enthusiasm.

'Maybe she's changed. I mean, wouldn't it be great if she really wanted the two of you to get close?'

Danielle's eyes had clouded for a second, but then

she'd shaken her head. 'I'm too old to believe in miracles, Ginny.'

'Well, then, let her think she's getting some mileage out of you, the same as when you were kids.' Ginny had grinned impishly. 'You'll be getting yours, too. A summer abroad—on a film set, no less!'

But the final straw had fallen that afternoon. The phone had been ringing as Danielle came in the door. It had been Aunt Helen, calling from Arizona. Her aunt hadn't let her get a word in before she'd started saying how happy she was that her two girls were going to spend the summer together, and then Uncle John had got on the phone, saying how pleased he was that his girls were still pals, that he hadn't seen Helen look so bright and chipper since her heart attack.

'You have to go now,' Ginny had said innocently. 'I mean, how can you let your aunt down?'

'I can't, I guess,' Danielle had said.

But she could have, she thought now, shifting in the hard plastic chair at New York's Kennedy Airport. The simple truth was that she'd hidden behind Ginny's urgings and Aunt Helen's delight—she'd wanted to accept Val's offer all along, she just hadn't wanted to admit it to herself. Teachers were as underpaid in Missouri as they were everywhere else. This might be the only chance she'd have to spend eight weeks in France, at least in the foreseeable future.

'Ladies and gentlemen, good day. We are now ready to begin boarding Air France's Flight 010 direct to Nice. Will first-class passengers kindly. . .'

Danielle's heartbeat quickened in anticipation. She rose, clutching her shoulder-bag in one hand and her carry-on in the other. Her ticket was for a seat well in the rear of the plane, but it didn't hurt to begin moving towards the gate. The flight would be crowded, she could see that. There were hordes of vacationers jostling each other, lots of squalling babies and——

She stumbled to a sudden halt, her gaze inexorably drawn to the first-class passengers as they moved towards the gate. There was only a handful of them, but the man who'd shared the lounge with her earlier stood out clearly.

Perhaps it was the way he held himself, with a reckless kind of arrogance, or the angle of his shoulders, squared as if he were ready to take on the world. Or was it something far less obvious, some subconscious awareness that drew her to him as it had from the start, some message carried in the darkness of her blood?

Danielle's breath caught as he came to a sudden stop. The crowd parted and surged past him as he stood still, his head cocked as if listening. He turned slowly, his eyes scanning the huge room, and an electric tingle danced along her spine.

She knew, without question, why his eyes searched every face. He was looking for her, waiting for her.

She took a step back, blending quickly into the crowd. Her heart raced as she watched him.

'*Mesdames et monsieurs. . .*'

The crowd surged past her, blocking him from view. When she looked again, he was gone.

CHAPTER TWO

THE plane was as crowded as Danielle had expected. Passengers jammed the tourist-class aisles, some peering at seat numbers, others elbowing each other aside as they tried to get at the overhead storage hatches.

Her seat was in the rear of the plane, the centre seat in a group of three, and the other two were already occupied.

'Excuse me,' she said to the heavy-set woman on the aisle side. The woman glanced up, then nodded. Her face was shiny with sweat.

'Are we going to take off soon, do you think?' she whispered as Danielle struggled past her.

Danielle smiled politely. 'I hope so.'

The man in the window seat grumbled something. 'We'd damned well better,' he said. 'I've got a connection to make at Nice.'

But their take-off was delayed for almost an hour. Technical problems, the captain announced over the loudspeaker. The phrase sent the heavy-set woman into little gasps of anguish and the irritated man into even louder grumbles. By the time the plane was finally airborne, he was fairly twitching. But as soon as the 'fasten seatbelt' signs blinked off, he put back his seat, closed his eyes, and fell soundly asleep.

To Danielle's surprise, her white-knuckled companion on the aisle side did the same. The woman's head lolled back and, within minutes, she was snoring delicately.

Danielle sighed with relief. She'd been afraid the woman's nervousness would make her want to chatter, and the last thing she felt like doing was making small talk. There was a dull pain in her temple that threatened to work itself into a full-blown headache. And she was as tense as a coiled spring. She couldn't stop thinking about what had happened at the boarding gate. The scene kept playing in her mind like a loop of film that would run over and over until it wore out.

There had to be a way to make sense out of it. She knew what seemed to have happened: the man she'd met in the lounge had expected to see her at the boarding gate. When she hadn't appeared, he'd looked for her.

End of story.

But she knew that it hadn't been that simple. She'd felt the intensity of his gaze across the room. And then there had been her own reaction, that thrumming pulse of her blood——

'Excuse me.'

The low-pitched masculine voice startled her. Her pulse leaped as she looked up. But it was only the man from the window seat, apologising as he made his way past her to the aisle. Danielle sighed and laid her head back. Who else would it have been? The stranger wasn't going to come looking for her. He was hidden behind the curtains that separated first-class from the rest of the plane. And anyway, why would he want to find her? He'd probably forgotten the whole thing by now.

Which was precisely what she would do, she told herself firmly as she dredged the Frommer's guidebook that Ginny had given her from the depths of her shoulder-bag. She'd be in France soon, and seeing all the lovely old places she'd read about would be a dream come true.

She was deep in a description of Versailles when the woman beside her yawned loudly.

'My goodness,' she said with a little laugh, 'did I fall asleep? I didn't think I'd——' Her breath caught. 'Excuse me,' she whispered as she leaned heavily across

Danielle and stared out of the window, 'do you see that wing? Is it supposed to look like that?'

Danielle followed the woman's trembling finger and then she smiled. 'It looks fine to me,' she said gently.

Her neighbour touched her tongue to her lips. 'Are you sure? I—I know it sounds silly, but I thought it looked loose. Just at the end there, you see? Where the metal is so thin.'

Danielle smiled again. 'I'm sure it's fine.'

'Well, if you think so. . .' The woman touched her tongue to her lips again. 'I won't bother you any more. I'm sure you'd rather read your book.'

Danielle sighed. 'You didn't bother me at all,' she said, closing the Frommer.

'Are you sure? Well, that's nice to hear. I'm Alice Davis. Have you been abroad before? I have. One time. Two, really, if you count the trip I took to Bermuda. But that's not going abroad, is it? Not like Europe, I mean. I always say. . .'

Hours later, when the plane finally touched down at the Nice-Côte d'Azur Airport, Danielle almost groaned with relief. Somehow she managed to smile at Alice, who'd talked, almost non-stop, across the entire Atlantic.

'Aren't you getting off?' Alice asked as she eased her bulky self into the aisle.

Danielle looked at the passengers already crowding the narrow space and shook her head.

'I'll wait,' she said. 'It doesn't look as if anyone's going anywhere for a while anyway.'

Alice laughed. 'You're probably smart to avoid the crowd. But I can hardly wait to get my feet on solid ground again. And my niece is waiting—I haven't seen her in a year. You understand.'

Danielle smiled and waved her hand as Alice moved into the queue, and then she settled back into her seat.

The man in the window seat had already trampled her toes in his rush to disembark, muttering that he'd never make his connecting flight, thanks to the delay back in New York.

Everyone was in a rush to go somewhere, she thought with a sigh, everyone except her. She had no plane to catch, no one waiting for her at the gate.

'I won't be able to meet you, Danni,' Val had said when Danielle had phoned to confirm her arrival. 'It's a working day. But you won't mind, will you?'

Danielle had said she wouldn't. But the truth was that there was something awfully lonely about stepping off a plane in a strange country with no one to greet you...

Unless he was waiting, unless he was, even now, watching eagerly for her, scanning each face with those dark blue eyes.

Quickly, Danielle rose and picked up her carry-on and shoulder-bag. Alice had been right, she thought as she pushed into the aisle, there was really no sense in sitting here. She might as well get going.

The Nice-Côte d'Azur terminal was disappointing. It was foolish, she knew, but she'd expected something more exotic than this crowded, noisy place that reminded her of airport terminals everywhere. People were jabbering at each other as they lined up around the baggage carousel, but the jabbering was all in English. Well, this *was* the height of the tourist season, that was what it said in her Frommer—the little she'd managed to read of it, anyway. And the Côte d'Azur was Mecca to both the British and the Americans.

There was a long, slow-moving queue at Customs. Danielle gave the inspector a hesitant smile, but he barely glanced up. He seemed bored, even disinterested, as he held out his hand for her papers.

'How long will you be in France?' he asked. 'Are you here on business or pleasure?'

His English was heavily accented. Without thinking, Danielle responded in French, and suddenly his face was wreathed in smiles.

'Ah, *mademoiselle,*' he said, and he burst into the swift, musical language she had studied and loved for so many years.

French, she thought, he's speaking real French, and suddenly her heart raced with excitement. She was really here! She was in Europe and the summer lay ahead, the long weeks beckoning like unwrapped gifts lying beneath a Christmas tree.

Danielle dragged her suitcase to the car-rental counter. Her breath hissed from her lungs as she eased it down and flexed her hand wearily. She would be in Ste Agathe soon, with Val. What she'd told Ginny was true—she didn't believe in miracles and she didn't expect one—but it was going to be nice to see Val again.

There was so much to catch up on—Val probably had dozens of fantastic stories to tell. While Danielle had been drumming French into unwilling adolescent heads, her glamorous cousin had been burning a swath through New York and Hollywood. She'd been everywhere and done everything—she'd even broken two engagements and who knew how many hearts. Danielle smiled to herself. Listening to Val would be like reading a glossy magazine.

As for the things she'd tell Val, well, there wasn't all that much to talk about. Danielle liked teaching, but Val would probably think it dull. Her smile dimmed a little. She could tell her about Eddie, of course, how kind he had been, how good.

Eddie. It was the first time she'd thought of him in hours. But that was understandable. Today had been such a rush. First Ginny's old car had had to be coaxed into starting. She'd had to race to make the plane at St

Louis. And then there'd been all that foolishness at the Air France lounge.

But that was all behind her now. Besides, just because she hadn't thought about Eddie, it didn't mean she'd forgotten him.

She never would, she thought as she moved slowly forward in the queue. Eddie had been the gentlest man she'd ever known. And he'd loved her very much. She'd loved him too, although not quite the way he'd wanted. But he'd made her feel needed, and perhaps knowing someone needed you was enough. Heaven knew she'd tried to feel what he felt, but it just hadn't happened. Not even his kisses had made her heart race the way it had when she'd seen the stranger searching for her at the boarding gate.

God! What was she thinking? She couldn't compare her feelings for Eddie to anything else. She'd loved Eddie, she'd——

'*Mademoiselle?*' Danielle looked up. The clerk at the car-rental counter gave her a polite smile. 'How may I help you?'

Danielle fumbled in her shoulder-bag for her rental agreement. 'You have a car reserved for me,' she said. 'A compact. My name is Danielle Nichols, and I made arrangements in——'

She broke off and stared at the clerk, who was looking down at the rental contract and shaking her head.

'*Alors*, I am afraid I have not.'

'Have not what?' Danielle asked slowly, her eyes locked on the woman's face.

'A car, *mademoiselle*.' The clerk looked up and smiled sadly. 'We have none for you.'

'But—but of course you have.' Danielle tapped her finger against the rental agreement. 'Don't you see what this says? I have a car reserved for this day. Here's my name and flight number, the time of my arrival. . .'

'*Oui*. That is exactly so. And you have arrived more than one and one half hours late.' The woman smiled. 'You had a car at a discounted price until twenty minutes ago.'

'You mean I'm too late?' Danielle sighed. 'Well, then, I'll pay the regular price. Not that I think that's right, you understand. But——'

'There are no cars, Mademoiselle Nichols. Not at any price.'

Danielle shook her head. 'That can't be. I *must* have a car. I have to drive to Ste Agathe. I don't know any other way to reach it.'

'I am terribly sorry, *mademoiselle*. Perhaps you can take a taxi. There is a stand, just outside. And then, tomorrow. . .'

A long argument later, Danielle snatched up her suitcase and marched towards the exit doors. Tomorrow, she thought furiously. What good was that? She had to reach Ste Agathe today. Well, she'd just have to take a taxi, although who knew what it would cost? Val had sent her a cramped, hand-drawn map and, for all she knew, Ste Agathe was miles from here. The trip would probably cost a fortune.

Her footsteps slowed, then stopped. She should have asked the clerk what the fare would be. How many francs were there to a dollar, anyway? Five? Six? For that matter, how many francs did she have in her wallet? Not a lot; the guidebook had said it was better to change your money at a bank at your destination.

'For God's sake, are you just going to stand there?'

The man's voice was deep, a little husky, and touched with impatience. Danielle's mouth went dry as his hand closed around her arm. No, she thought, no, it couldn't be.

But she knew it was he even before she turned towards

him. It was the man she'd run from on another continent. 'What are you doing here?' she said.

It was a stupid thing to say. But she couldn't think of anything else. Besides, what *was* he doing here? He should have left the terminal a long time ago.

He laughed. 'Saving your tail,' he said, 'that's what I'm doing here. It's getting to be a habit.'

His eyes met hers, but there was no electric charge in them this time. There was, instead, a look of faint amusement, and she realised suddenly that that was what she'd heard in his voice, too.

He wasn't impatient with her, he was laughing at her, and not for the first time. The realisation was infuriating.

'What a gracious way to put it,' she said coldly. 'But I'm happy to say I don't need your help.'

'Really? And just how in hell are you going to get to Ste Agathe?'

Danielle twisted free of his grasp. 'I'll manage,' she said, and then she frowned. 'How did you know——?'

'I overheard your conversation at the car-rental counter.'

Her chin lifted. 'Are you in the habit of spying on women?'

He laughed softly. 'Such ego, Miss Nichols. Have you got secrets to hide?'

Danielle felt her cheeks grow pink. Easy, she told herself. Don't let him shake you. Thanks to him, you've already played the fool once.

'No,' she said calmly. 'I just find it strange that we would bump into each other again, especially since I saw you looking for me at Kennedy. You were——'

She broke off in confusion. His eyes darkened and a little smile tilted at the corners of his mouth.

'Was I?' he said softly. 'How could you tell?'

So much for playing it cool. What was she going to say now? She couldn't think of anything that wouldn't make things worse—which was ridiculous. There was no reason to be so damned tongue-tied. If he just—if he just wouldn't look at her that way, if he'd just back off so she could catch her breath. . .

Stop it, she told herself firmly, and she tilted her head back and gave him a dazzling smile. 'It's been lovely,' she said, 'being charmed by you twice in one day. But you'll have to forgive me—I'm in a rush. So if you'd just step aside. . .'

He grinned. 'At least you're doing better now than you were a few hours ago.'

Danielle stared at him. 'What's that supposed to mean?'

'It means,' he said, 'that you seem to have decided I'm not the big bad wolf in disguise.' He sighed and reached for her suitcase. 'The trouble is, it's too late for me to appreciate it. I'm tired as hell—I spent damned near the last twenty-four hours in the air, and I just made a call and found out it was all for nothing.'

'Will you please put down my suitcase?'

'Don't give me a hard time, lady. I told you, I'm wiped out.'

Danielle's eyebrows rose. 'That's hardly my problem. Just because you——'

'Your problem,' he said, 'is reaching Ste Agathe, which happens to be exactly where I'm headed.'

His answer stopped her dead. 'Ste Agathe?' She looked at him. His expression was unreadable, and after a moment, she shook her head. 'I don't believe you.'

He muttered something sharp and succinct under his breath, and then he dropped her suitcase to the floor.

'Look,' he said, putting his hands on his hips, 'I'm flattered. Really. I like playing cat and mouse. Hell, any other time I'd be delighted to go on for hours.' His eyes narrowed. 'But not now. I told you, I'm tired. And I'm irritable. All I want to do is get to my rooms and take a shower.'

Danielle stared at him. 'Cat and mouse? I haven't the slightest idea what you're——'

'Come on, don't give me that. I make a move and you parry with a cold shoulder. It's a sexy little game—hell, I didn't think you knew it, at first. But you do—and you're damned good at it.' He moved closer to her, and the slow smile she remembered all too well angled across his mouth. 'Of course,' he said in a husky whisper, 'we could kill two birds with one stone. You must be as tired as I am. Why don't we go someplace quiet and climb into a shower together?'

Colour flared in Danielle's cheeks and she reached for her suitcase, snatching it up despite its weight. 'Not if you were the last man on earth.'

Laughter lit his eyes again. 'Your choice, sweetheart. Too bad. You would have been great company.'

'The taxi driver who's going to take me to Ste Agathe is the only company I want.'

The man grinned. 'No problem,' he said, jamming a pair of dark glasses on his nose. 'Enjoy your ride. Do yourself a favour and tell the driver to take the road to Mont Abat. That should cut off a few kilometres. And tell him you know the law, that you don't have to pay his gas or share the ride with anyone else. Of course, you'll have to pay his fare both ways.'

Danielle swallowed. 'Both ways? But——'

'It's a long trip, Miss Nichols. You don't think these guys work for nothing, do you?'

She hesitated. 'I—I don't suppose you know what the fare will be?'

'Not to the centime, no. But eight hundred francs ought to do it.'

'Eight hundred. . .' She turned pale. 'But that's more than a hundred and thirty dollars.'

'Unless he refuses to go via Mont Abat, in which case you'll add on another fifty or sixty francs. Oh, and you'll have to add on a tip, of course.'

'Of course,' she said weakly. Slowly, she set her suitcase down beside her. Eight hundred francs. That was almost as much as the cost of renting a car for two weeks. It was an enormous amount of money; it would put a dent in her careful budget, and this was only her first day.

She drew a breath and looked up at the man again. She had the feeling he was watching her closely but it was impossible to be sure, now that his eyes were hidden behind the dark glasses.

'Are you—are you really going to Ste Agathe?' she asked.

His lips drew back from his teeth. 'That's what I said.'

'But—but I don't know you. I mean. . .'

'Would a formal introduction make you feel better, Miss Nichols?'

'I know this must seem very funny to you,' Danielle said coldly, 'but I'm not in the habit of going off with strangers.'

'We're not strangers, though. We've had two absolutely delightful conversations, we shared a plane ride. . .' He held up his hands in surrender when he saw the look on Danielle's face. 'You're quite right,' he said solemnly. 'Two people who are about to set off on a journey together should at least know each other's names. Anyway, I already know yours. I suppose you're entitled to the same courtesy.' He made a sweeping bow. 'Lee Bradford, at your service, mam'selle.'

Something in the way he offered his name gave her pause. 'Should I—am I supposed to know your name, or something?'

'Or something,' he said with a quick smile.

Was he an actor? Was that why he was going to Ste Agathe? He was certainly handsome enough.

She drew in her breath. 'I'm sorry,' she said, 'but I'm afraid——'

'I'm a racer.'

Danielle looked blank. 'You can't be. Jockeys are short, aren't they?'

He reached up slowly and pulled off his glasses. There was laughter in his eyes again. 'Cars,' he said softly. 'Race cars. I'm a driver, Miss Nichols.'

Race cars, she thought. Of course. It was easy to imagine him behind the wheel of a powerful car, the wind whipping into his face and the engine growling.

'I'm sorry,' she said, 'I'm not very. . .'

The look of amusement left his face. It was, she thought, like glimpsing the real features behind a mask, but before she could quite grasp what it was she'd thought she'd seen, the arrogant expression was back.

'No,' he said, picking up her suitcase, 'you're not.' He started towards the doors as Danielle stared after him, and then he turned and looked at her. 'Well? Are you coming or not?'

She caught her bottom lip between her teeth. 'I—I don't know. Maybe I can get a car at another counter. Maybe I should telephone. . .'

Lee Bradford sighed and dropped her luggage to the floor. 'All right,' he said, walking towards her, 'let's get it over with.'

Danielle stared at him. 'I don't understand.'

He smiled as his hands clasped her shoulders. 'Yes, you do,' he said softly. 'You've been wondering about this from the minute I walked into that lounge in New York.' His eyes swept over her face and settled on her mouth. 'Maybe if we get the suspense out of the way, we can get to Ste Agathe before next week.'

She knew what he was going to do a second before it

happened, but it was still too late. Her hands came up and pressed against his chest as he bent his head towards hers.

'No,' she said frantically, 'you can't do that.'

If only she hadn't protested, she thought later, if only she hadn't said anything or done anything, it might have ended there. His kiss was only meant to tease her, she knew that even as she fought against it.

His mouth only brushed hers lightly, but when her lips parted to vent her protest, everything changed. Lee's mouth closed over hers and then his arms tightened around her.

Danielle whimpered softly as he drew her to him. She felt the quick race of his heart beneath her hands and the answering race of her own, and then his lips moved against hers. Suddenly time and reality dropped away.

She had no idea how long it was before his hands cupped her shoulders again and he thrust her from him. They stood staring at each other, locked in a silence so thick it seemed almost palpable. Then, before Danielle could speak, Lee let out his breath and turned away.

'OK,' he said evenly, 'that's out of the way. Can you manage your carry-on yourself, or shall I take it?'

Danielle shook her head. 'I—I. . .'

Her words faded and Lee swung towards her. 'Last chance, little girl,' he said. His voice sounded angry, almost fierce. 'Maybe you ought to forget about Ste Agathe and get on the next plane back to the States.'

It was, she thought with sudden, terrible clarity, probably the best advice anyone had ever given her.

But instead of taking it, Danielle swung the strap of her carry-on over her shoulder. 'Where's your car, Mr Bradford?' she asked with determined coolness, and without another word she followed him out into the hot Mediterranean sun.

CHAPTER THREE

LEE BRADFORD's car was a low-slung, gleaming black machine that looked as if it were moving even when it was standing still. He tossed Danielle's suitcase and carry-on into the boot, then unlocked the passenger door and gave her a casual salute.

'Your taxi, Miss Nichols.'

Danielle looked from him to the car. The interior looked barely large enough for two. The leather bucket seats were close to the ground, which meant her legs, bare beneath her light summer dress, would probably be stuck out almost straight under the dashboard.

She turned and glanced towards the taxi stand and the long queue of travellers waiting there. Eight hundred francs, she thought. It was a lot of money, and who knew how long it would take until it was her turn? But perhaps it was worth it. Perhaps——

'Having second thoughts, little girl?'

Laughter danced in Bradford's voice. Danielle met his derisive glance. God, the man was insufferable! First he'd expected her to be an easy pick-up; when she hadn't been, he'd decided she was a naïve little thing—probably because his ego wouldn't let him think otherwise.

Probably, she suddenly thought, because that was how she'd acted.

Her head came up and she forced herself to meet his smile with an aloof one of her own. 'Not at all,' she said calmly. 'I was just wondering why anyone would drive a thing like this. It doesn't look very comfortable.'

He laughed as he went around to the driver's side and slipped behind the wheel. 'Comfort hasn't a thing to do with it.'

He was right, of course. It hadn't, and Danielle knew it. The car was made for speed. But speed was impossible along the heavily trafficked roads leading from the airport. She could feel Lee's barely contained impatience: the fingers of his left hand tapped a restive tattoo on the steering-wheel while his right clenched and unclenched on the gear shifter. He changed position in his seat, easing his long legs under the dashboard, then leaned forward and pressed a button on the instrument panel. A motor whined softly, and part of the roof overhead slid back.

A luxuriant floral scent filled the car. Danielle drew a deep breath. 'What's that lovely smell?' she said softly.

Bradford glanced at her, then at the road. 'Flowers. All kinds of flowers. And herbs—rosemary, thyme, sage—Provence is like an enormous garden. Why don't you sit back and enjoy it?'

'I am.'

He smiled. 'No, you're not. You're too busy trying to keep your skirt over your knees. I assure you, Miss Nichols, I've seen women with more than their legs bare.' His teeth flashed in a quick grin. 'You might as well relax.'

She stared at him, then looked quickly back at the road. If only she could think of some clever reply, if only she could turn his teasing jibes back on him. But she'd tried that, and it had only backfired. The best thing to do was just to keep still.

Traffic was still heavy, but Lee took advantage of every opening in the clotted flow, surging in and out of the stream of cars with quick bursts of speed. The car seemed as impatient as its driver. The engine growled like a mean thing trapped in a cage, occasionally rising to what seemed to her ears an angry scream. Danielle glanced at Lee's profile. He looked tense; his mouth was hard, his jaw was set with concentration.

Finally, they shot past the last automobile. His foot came down harder on the accelerator and the car leaped eagerly ahead. They were speeding along a road so narrow and winding that she could only hope they would meet no car coming in the other direction. Carefully, Danielle glanced at Lee Bradford. All his attention was on the road, but there was nothing tense about him now. He was sitting back almost lazily, his left hand lying loosely on the steering-wheel, his right on the gear shifter. He looked relaxed, but she knew he was totally in command of the swift-moving car which responded to his touch, purring beneath his hand like a satisfied cat.

Or like a contented woman.

The thought came swiftly and unexpectedly. At first, she was afraid she'd spoken aloud. But another look at him assured her she hadn't. His eyes were still on the road, and there was a look on his face that told her he was as much caught up in the pleasure of the swift-moving car as she was in thinking about him.

Danielle felt a sudden sweep of irrational anger. 'Must you drive so fast?' she said sharply.

He glanced at her. 'We're not going fast at all, Miss Nichols.' His eyes went to the speedometer, as did hers. 'We've barely hit ninety.'

Ninety! How could they have reached such speed without her even noticing? Had she left her senses behind in the States? she thought, and her irritation grew.

'I'd appreciate it if you'd slow down, Mr Bradford.'

Lee laughed. 'What's the matter, little girl? Are you scared?'

'No.' Her voice was cool, which amazed her, because his assessment was right on target. 'You don't scare me, you amaze me. Why should a grown man want to risk his neck playing such foolish games?'

A muscle knotted in his jaw. 'High-stake games are the only ones worth playing,' he said softly, but even as his spoke his foot eased on the pedal and the car slowed to a more respectable seventy-five. 'But you're right, Miss Nichols. All you signed on for was a ride to Ste Agathe, not the Grand Prix.' They rode in silence, and then he looked at her. 'I take it you've never been to the Côte d'Azur before.'

Was he going to try and make pleasant conversation? If he was, he'd end up talking to himself.

'No,' Danielle said, staring straight ahead.

'Are you on vacation, then?'

'Yes.'

He sighed. 'And you're going to Ste Agathe as your first stop.'

'Yes.'

The road lifted ahead, uncoiling like a grey ribbon as it entered the mountains. Bradford down-shifted and the engine hummed softly in accord.

'Do you have a dog?'

Despite herself, Danielle turned and stared at him. 'What?'

'A dog,' he said patiently. 'Do you have one?'

Her brows drew together. 'No.'

Bradford shrugged. 'A pity,' he said softly. 'I was going to ask if you still beat him.'

Her eyes fastened on his impassive profile. '*If* I had a dog, I'd never beat him. Besides, that's a stupid question to ask someone. You can't give a "yes" or a "no" answer to something like that, you have to. . .' Her voice faded as he began to chuckle. Danielle glared at him for a few seconds, and then a smile tugged at the corners of her mouth. '*Touché*, Mr Bradford.'

'Lee.' He glanced at her and smiled. 'You might as well call me that. Ste Agathe has a population that would fit into a sardine tin. Calling me Mr Bradford is going to mark you as an outsider.'

Danielle shifted towards him. 'Is it really small?'

Lee nodded. 'It is—or it was, until the film crew arrived.'

'You know about the film they're shooting there?'

He grinned. 'Oh, yes, Miss Nichols. I do, indeed.'

'Danielle,' she said without thinking.

His eyes met hers. 'What's that?'

'Danielle. It's my name. If I'm going to call you by your first name, you——' She broke off and a light blush rose in her cheeks. 'You knew that was my name.'

The slow smile she already knew well curved across Lee's mouth. 'Yes,' he said softly, 'I did. But I wanted to hear you ask me to say it.'

Their eyes met. Danielle's breath caught; her name had become a caress when he used it. And the way he was looking at her made her feel—made her feel. . .

She turned away quickly and stared straight ahead. They were climbing higher and higher into the mountains—she could see the rocky drop to the valley. It was a sight she'd always longed to see, but now it was all a blur. The only thing she could see clearly was the man seated beside her.

She lay her head back and inhaled deeply. What was the matter with her? Exhaustion, probably. One way or another, she'd spent most of the past day in the air. And she was wary about seeing Val again. Yes. Exhaustion, that was it. That was why she felt so—so confused, so vulnerable. It had nothing to do with Lee Bradford. Nothing. . .

'. . .history buff?'

Danielle moistened her lips with her tongue. 'Sorry,' she said brightly. 'I was thinking about—about Ste Agathe. Did you ask me something?'

He smiled. 'Yes. I asked if you were a history buff.'

She shook her head. 'No,' she said slowly, 'not especially. Why do you ask?'

Lee shrugged his shoulders. 'Ste Agathe doesn't get

many tourists. The ones who come are usually interested in the walls.' He glanced at her. 'The Roman walls,' he said, 'the ones left standing around the western portion of the town.'

'I didn't know there were any.'

'It's about all the town has going for it. Well, that and its antiquity. It's a handsome little place—if you're into fifteenth-century houses and quiet lanes.'

Danielle smiled. 'I gather you're not.'

Lee shrugged again. 'They're all right, I suppose.' His hand flexed on the steering-wheel, and she noticed how lightly it seemed to lie there, how little effort it took for him to control the powerful automobile. 'But I'm used to a different kind of life. Racing circuits tend to be where the lights are brightest. Monte Carlo, Le Mans, Mexico City—that's what I'm used to.' He grinned at her. 'Wexler says Ste Agathe's peaceful. But I keep telling him that a tomb is peaceful, too.'

Danielle smiled in return. Yes, she thought, looking at him, a man like this would be unhappy tucked way in a quiet village. She knew little about Lee Bradford, but what she sensed told her that he craved excitement, that he needed it as some men needed food or drink. There'd be no bright lights in a place like Ste Agathe, no fast cars, no beautiful women to drape themselves around him as she knew they must in the real world.

She blinked. *Wexler*? Did he mean Barney Wexler? It had to be. How many Wexlers would you find in a place the size of Ste Agathe?

'Lee?' He glanced at her and she touched her tongue to her lips. 'Are you with the film crew?'

He sighed and looked back at the road. 'Unfortunately, the answer's yes.'

Danielle frowned. 'But you said you're a racing driver.'

'Yeah.' He shifted uncomfortably. 'That's what I keep telling myself.'

'I don't understand. If you're a driver. . .'

He laughed softly. 'Forgive my immodesty, love, but I'm not *a* driver, I'm *the* driver. Well, last year's, anyway, although I'm trying my damnedest to come out on top two years in a row. I had more championship points than anyone else, I won more races. . .' He looked at Danielle's blank face and laughed again. 'You're bad for my ego, do you know that? You keep looking at me as if I were talking Martian.'

'I'm sorry. But I told you, I don't know anything about. . .'

Lee sighed. 'Neither does Wexler, which is why he asked me to serve as technical adviser on his film. Somebody introduced us at a party in New York, I guess it was. And then we bumped into each other again at a bash in Zurich.'

'Zurich,' Danielle repeated. She watched him, remembering what he'd said about speaking Martian. He'd meant it as a jest, but it was true enough. They might as well have come from different worlds, she thought, and a strange sadness tightened her throat.

He grinned. 'I think it was Zurich. Hell, maybe it was Barcelona. I'm not really sure. Not that it matters—I just wish I'd been sober when Wexler tendered the invitation.' Danielle's eyebrows rose and his grin became a rueful smile. 'That's what I tell myself, anyway. It makes me feel better to think I was drunk when I agreed to sign on as his technical adviser.'

Danielle shook her head. 'I really don't understand at all. If you didn't want to accept, why did you?'

'Who the hell knows? Equal parts stupidity and boredom, maybe.' His mouth turned down. 'My business manager thought it might be time I tried something else. Besides, my principal sponsor's money is in this film, and I have damned near a month and a half before my next race.' He laughed softly. 'Believe me, I'm looking forward to it.'

She smiled. 'You make it sound like—like——'

'Like heaven and hell combined,' he said. 'When I'm on the tour, I want to be somewhere else. And when I'm somewhere else, I want to be on the tour.'

'You lead a strange life,' she said with a smile.

He shrugged. 'It's been interesting, anyway.'

'And the film? Have you enjoyed working on it?'

Lee shrugged. 'It's different, I have to say that.'

She smiled. 'Yes, I'm sure it is. Working on a movie sounds pretty exciting.'

'Believe me, it isn't.' He lifted his right hand and ran his fingers through his dark hair. 'But things will pick up by the end of the month. We'll be changing locations.'

Danielle looked at him in surprise. 'Changing locations?'

'Yeah. Wexler wants to shoot some racing footage in Monaco. I can hardly wait—it'll be good to get behind the wheel of ——'

'Monaco? But I thought. . .' Danielle drew a deep breath. 'There must be a mistake. Val told me she'd be here all summer. She said——'

Lee stared at her. 'Val?'

'Yes. Valerie Cummings, do you know her? She's——'

He laughed softly. 'Oh, yes, I know her, all right. You might say we're old acquaintances.'

Something in his voice made Danielle look up sharply. The sun was shining directly overhead, and it seemed to beat down on Lee Bradford's face. But his eyes were on the road ahead, and she could see only his profile. Suddenly, he turned towards her.

'Of course,' he said, 'I should have guessed. You're Val's cousin.'

Danielle nodded. 'That's right. But how did you——?'

Lee's mouth narrowed. 'She said you'd show up, but I didn't believe her.'

'I'm sorry, but I don't. . .'

His eyes fixed on her face. 'She said all she had to do was tell you she needed you and you'd come running.' He paused. 'And it looks as if she was right.'

'Did she, really?' Her voice was cold.

'The little Mississippi cousin,' Lee said. 'Well, well, well.'

'Missouri,' she said, even more coldly, 'I'm from Missouri, not Mississippi.'

'Does it really matter?' For some reason, he sounded angry. 'Val's little farm girl. . .'

'I am none of those,' Danielle said curtly. 'I'm not Val's, I'm not from a farm, and I'm not a little girl. And I'll thank you to keep all three in mind. I——' She broke off as a white shape stepped delicately into the road. 'Lee!' Her voice rose in horror. 'Look out—there's a goat!'

Lee stepped down hard on the brakes. The acrid stench of burning rubber and the squeal of the tyres grabbing for purchase on the road surface filled the air. The car skidded across the narrow road, coming to rest on the dirt shoulder.

Danielle stared out of the window and her stomach rose into her throat as a stone, dislodged by the tyres, clattered down the steep hillside behind them. Picking up speed, it rolled towards the edge of the cliff and plunged over the side on its way to the valley floor, hundreds of feet below.

Silence filled the car, and then Lee was beside her, his fingers brushing lightly against her breasts as he unbuckled her seatbelt.

'Danielle.' His arm closed around her and he drew her towards him. 'Danielle. Are you OK?'

She nodded. 'Yes,' she whispered, 'I'm fine. I just—I just. . .'

He put his finger under her chin and tilted her face up to his. 'Are you sure? No bumps? No bruises?'

She shook her head as his hand skimmed lightly over her cheeks and her temples, then moved into her hair.

'No. Honestly, I didn't bang against anything. I. . .' She swallowed. His arm was still around her, holding her close to him. The silence seemed to grow louder. The scent of wild flowers filled the narrow space, making her dizzy. There was another scent mixing with the flowers—Lee's scent, a heady combination of sun and sweat and maleness.

'Danielle.'

He whispered her name. The sound of it made a slow pulse begin to beat deep within her.

'Please,' she said. His arm tightened around her; his dark head bent towards hers. 'Lee. . .' She swallowed. 'The goat—is he all right? Did we hit him?'

He looked at her for a long moment, and then he began to smile. 'You see?' he said softly, his blue eyes sweeping over her face. 'I was right. You *are* a farm girl; you're more worried about the goat than you are about me.'

'What do you mean? I. . .'

His eyes fell to her mouth. 'You've yet to ask me if *I'm* all right.'

'Haven't I? I'm sorry. But I thought—I mean, you seem fine.'

Why did he have to keep looking at her mouth that way? It was—it was like a kiss; she could almost feel his lips moving against hers, she could almost taste his honeyed sweetness, the nectar of the flowers.

Lee smiled. 'I *am* fine,' he said, touching his finger to

her lips, lightly tracing their outline. 'And so's the goat. He's probably around that curve, telling all his friends in Ste Agathe about his close brush with death.'

It seemed hard to breathe, harder still to concentrate on anything but the feel of his hand.

'Is—is Ste Agathe nearby?'

'Mmm.'

'Then we—we can get out and walk. We can. . .'

Lee cupped her face in his hand. 'Is that what you want to do?' he said softly.

Danielle's head was spinning. What did she want? she thought desperately. An hour or two ago, she'd have said she wanted to reach St Agathe and never have to lay eyes on Lee Bradford again. And that was how she'd felt again, just before the accident.

Now, as he held her in his arms, she wasn't quite so certain.

Lee murmured her name again and she raised her eyes to his. In the close confines of the car, they might have been the only people in the universe. He was going to kiss her. She knew he was, just as she knew she could stop him. He'd told her as much; all she had to do was tell him she wanted to get out of the car. But she couldn't. She couldn't. She——

With bone-jarring suddenness, the door was wrenched open. Danielle blinked as if awakening from a dream and looked past Lee's shoulder.

Her breath caught. Valerie was staring into the car, her face twisted with an emotion so ugly that it turned Danielle's blood cold.

'Val?' she said softly. Her cousin stared at her in silence. Danielle lifted her hands and put them against Lee's chest. 'Val,' she said again.

Lee let go of her slowly and turned towards the open door. Danielle watched as Valerie stared at him, and then the terrible expression fell away from her face and she reached towards him.

'Lee, darling,' she said breathlessly. 'We all heard the squeal of brakes. We thought. . .' She smiled as she bent forward and put her hands on either side of his face. 'But you're all right.'

'I'm fine.' Lee jerked his head towards Danielle. 'I brought you a surprise,' he said. 'Aren't you going to say hello to your cousin?'

Val's smile was bright enough to light a night sky. 'Not until I've finished saying hello to you, darling,' she whispered, and her mouth dropped to his.

Danielle watched in stunned silence, and then she turned away and stared blindly out of the window. The kiss seemed to go on forever, although, in her heart, she knew better.

It went on just long enough so that she couldn't mistake the truth.

Lee Bradford and her cousin were lovers.

CHAPTER FOUR

VALERIE peered into the smoky, gilt-framed mirror that hung on the wall of her sitting-room, frowned, then touched her finger lightly to her pale brows.

'The light's either glaring in here or it's a morgue,' she groused. 'It's hard to get my make-up on right. I keep asking Madame for brighter bulbs, but. . .'

Danielle nodded. 'It is rather bright, isn't it?' She sighed as she sank into the depths of an ancient, floral-print sofa. 'I thought you said this place was old and charming.'

'Well, it's old anyway,' her cousin said, smiling as she turned around, 'you have to admit that.'

Danielle stood quickly, looked at the sofa cushion, then lifted one high-heeled golden sandal out from beneath her. 'And cluttered,' she said, depositing the offending shoe on top of a magazine-littered table.

Val grinned. 'Like old times, right, Danni?'

'Yes,' Danielle said after a pause, 'like old times.'

'I meant to clean up a bit, but I've been awfully busy.' Val moved quickly through the boxy sitting-room, snatching up handfuls of discarded clothing. 'Anyway, what's the point? We'll be moving on in another week or so anyway, right?'

Danielle sighed as she collapsed on to the sofa again. 'I wish you'd told me about the location change, Val.'

'Why? It doesn't change anything; you'll still have a summer in Europe, only now you'll get to see more of it.' Val smiled prettily. 'And I'll still have my favourite cousin by my side.' Her heels tapped sharply against the wide-planked floor as she crossed the room and sat opposite Danielle. 'It really will be like old times, Danni. But at least you don't have to pick up after me, the way you did when we were kids.'

Danielle smiled pleasantly. 'I don't intend to,' she said.

Val glanced at her. 'Anyway,' she said after a pause, 'I thought we'd keep to separate rooms this time. You can take this sitting-room—the sofa opens into a bed that Madame swears is comfortable—and I'll keep the bedroom—how does that sound?'

Danielle shifted her weight on the creaking sofa. The hidden mattress was probably as uncomfortable as the cushions on which she sat, but the quick glimpse she'd had of Val's cluttered bedroom had been enough to make the decision easy.

'That sounds fine,' she said.

Val nodded. 'Good. You can put your things in the chest near the fireplace. And you can hang your dresses and stuff on the rod just behind the bathroom door.' She shrugged in apology. 'I meant to empty one of the wardrobes, but they're so full that—well, it seemed silly to take my things out of one place only to hang them in another. You don't mind, do you?'

Danielle got to her feet and walked to the chest of drawers. 'No,' she said, pulling open a drawer and peering inside, 'that'll be all right.'

'Good. That's settled, then.' The two women looked at each other and then Val smiled. 'So,' she said, 'how have you been?'

'Fine,' Danielle said, leaning back against the chest. 'And you?'

'Oh, fine. Just fine.'

They nodded foolishly at each other in the silence that followed, until Danielle cleared her throat. 'Ginny sends her regards.'

A little frown appeared between Val's pale green eyes. 'Who?'

'Ginny. Virginia Stanton, remember? She went to school with us.'

'Did she?' Val shrugged her shoulders. 'I can't seem to put the name with a face.'

There was another silence and Danielle cleared her throat again. 'I can hardly wait to get a look around Ste Agathe. The town looks charming—all those tiled roofs and timbered houses. And those walls—I had no idea there were Roman ruins here.'

Valerie yawned. 'Are there?' she said, and she yawned again. 'Sorry. I was out late last night.' She smiled as she brushed a fall of blonde hair from her eyes. 'A bunch of us went to this fantastic new disco in Nice—we had a blast.'

Silence stretched between the women again. Finally, Danielle sighed, walked to where her suitcase lay, and lifted it.

'I might as well unpack,' she said, carrying it across the room. 'My things are probably all wrinkled by now.'

'I should think you'd want to get some sleep before you did anythig else. Aren't you exhausted?'

'I should be, I know,' Danielle admitted as she heaved her suitcase to the top of the chest and unzipped it. 'But I'm not. I suppose it's all the excitement.'

'Yes. That was quite a close call you had.'

Something in Val's voice made Danielle look up. Her cousin was watching her through narrowed eyes. There was still a smile on her face, but it had undergone a subtle transformation.

'I wasn't thinking of the accident,' Danielle said quickly. 'I meant all the rest—the long flight, the time change, seeing you again. . .'

'And meeting Lee Bradford,' Val said, her eyes still

on Danielle. 'Don't tell me that wasn't exciting, too. After all, he's quite well known.'

Danielle lifted a stack of cotton sweaters from the suitcase and bent to the bottom drawer. Instinct told her this conversation was going to be unpleasant. Still, she'd been expecting it ever since she'd seen that moment of undisguised anger on Val's face when she'd found Danielle and Lee so close together in his car.

'Is he?' she asked casually. 'I'm afraid I'd never heard of him before.' She straightened up and burrowed in her suitcase for another pile of clothing. 'But then I never did follow sports very much.'

Val nodded. 'No, that's true, you didn't.' There was a creak of sagging springs and then the sound of her heels tapping across the floor. Danielle looked up as Val leaned against the wall next to the chest of drawers, her legs crossed delicately at the ankles, her arms folded over her rounded breasts. 'Still, I'd have thought even you would have heard of him, Danni. He's famous, like Mario Andretti.'

Danielle smiled. 'I don't know who that is either,' she said, closing the drawer and pulling open the one above it. 'Would you hand me those scarves? Thanks.'

Valerie watched Danielle in silence for a few moments and then she cleared her throat. 'You never did say how you and Lee met.'

'I told you—he overheard my conversation at the car-rental counter, and——'

'That hardly sounds like my little cousin,' Val said pleasantly. 'Letting a strange man talk her into his car.'

A slow flush rose to Danielle's cheeks. 'I'm not your *little* cousin any more,' she said quietly. 'Hadn't you noticed?'

'No,' Val said after a moment, her voice cold, 'you're not, are you?'

Danielle looked up. It would be foolish to get into an

argument; she hadn't come all this distance for that. And it would be especially foolish to argue over a man like Lee Bradford.

'As for accepting Lee's offer—well, I didn't have much choice. It was either that or spend a small fortune on a taxi. And it wasn't as if we were really strangers. . .'

Val's breath hissed as she inhaled sharply. 'What's that supposed to mean?'

It means I've put my foot in it, Danielle thought. She looked at her cousin and smiled brightly. 'We met in the VIP lounge at the airport in New York. A friend of mine—a friend of Ginny's, really—got me a pass. I wasn't supposed to be there, of course, not on a second-class ticket, but Ginny said——'

'Ah,' Val said, 'that's it, then. You met in the lounge and got to talking, and you told Lee you were coming here to visit me and he said he knew me, and——'

'Well, no. Actually, he was just being kind to a fellow American in distress. He heard me tell the clerk I had to get to Ste Agathe and he offered to help. Thank goodness he did. I mean, without him, I'd still be standing at the airport——'

Danielle clamped her lips together. She was running on like a fool, and all she was doing was digging the hole deeper and deeper. Why was she on the defensive? Her part in all this had been innocent.

'He's quite a Boy Scout, isn't he?' Val laughed, but it was an artificial sound. 'I wonder if he would have been as eager to offer a helping hand if you'd been twenty years older and sporting a moustache.'

A hanger slipped from Danielle's hands and clattered loudly against the wide-planked floor. 'Did your boss give you the afternoon off?' she said as she bent to retrieve it. 'That was nice of him. I hoped we'd have some time together today. It's been so long since we——'

'Lee should have been more careful on that road. He knows it twists and turns like a snake.'

'It wasn't his fault. The goat——'

'Yes. So he said.' Valerie stepped away from the wall and walked slowly to the centre of the room. She smiled coolly as she sat down on the sofa. 'What on earth was going on when I got to the car, Danni? Lee looked as if he was playing doctor.'

Danielle flushed. 'I suppose—I guess he was just trying to make sure I was all right.'

'Was he?'

It was a statement, not a question, and Danielle suspected it might be best not to respond. But the look in Val's eyes reminded her of a cat Aunt Helen had once owned. It had had a habit of purring gently, then reaching out and slashing you with its claws. 'Slap it sharply on the nose,' Aunt Helen had said, 'that's the only way to let the fool thing know you're on to its tricks.'

Danielle looked directly at her cousin. 'Listen, Val,' she said softly, 'I'm not in the least bit interested in your Mr Bradford. Have you got that straight?'

Val smiled. 'Aren't you?'

'No. He's all yours, believe me.'

The other woman's smile twisted a little. 'Yes, indeed he is.' She stared at Danielle, and then she sighed. 'I have your best interests at heart, Danni,' she said gently. 'How can I put this so your feelings won't be hurt? You see, I've known Lee for a while now; I've seen how foolish women can be when they're around him.' She smiled. 'It's not always their fault, of course. He's the kind of man who can't resist a pretty face. Not that I hold it against him. I mean, the racing circuit's loaded with groupies. And then, he's so good-looking. . .'

Colour flared in Danielle's cheeks. 'Val, I just told you——'

'We were in Cannes last weekend and he gave an autograph to some girl. She was awfully cute, and Lee just couldn't resist a little harmless flirting. It's like a game to him, you know?' Val tossed her head and laughed. 'Would you believe she phoned half the night? It kept both of us awake—not that we were really asleep,' she said, her brows arching delicately. 'If you know what I mean.'

'You don't have to paint pictures for me, Val,' Danielle said quietly. 'I'm not a child.'

The two cousins looked at each other for a few seconds and then Val got to her feet.

'I think you need a rest, Danni, no matter what you say. Take it from someone with experience, jet lag will catch up with you when you least expect it.' She crossed the room quickly and put her hand lightly on Danielle's arm. 'I just want you to know that I'm glad you're here,' she said, smiling.

The warmth in Val's voice surprised her. Danielle looked at her and smiled tentatively. 'Are you really?'

'Yes. Of course.'

Danielle's smile broadened. 'You know, on the plane coming over, I kept thinking that it's years since we spent any time together. I'm glad I decided to——'

'Mmm, so am I.' Val patted her absently, then moved past her to the mirror. 'Barney's French translator quit. Did I tell you?'

Danielle shook her head. 'No,' she said slowly, 'you didn't.'

'Well, he did, the awful man, and without any warning. Barney hasn't hired anyone else yet, so I've been working my butt off.' Their eyes met in the mirror. 'You will feel up to a bit of work by tomorrow, won't you?'

Danielle sighed. 'Sure.'

Val smiled and spun towards her. 'Good. Well, I'll see you later, then. Oh, by the way—if you want a shower, just remember to make it a quickie. There's not an awful lot of hot water. And don't worry if you oversleep. I'll ask Madame to send you a tray.'

'Don't bother doing that. I don't want to put your landlady to any trouble on my account.'

Val made a face. 'It's good practice to bother the dragon-lady from time to time. Anyway, she might as well earn what you'll be paying her.'

Danielle's hazel eyes widened. 'What do you mean?'

'She wants something for the extra linen and towels you'll be using.'

'But I thought——'

'I know. That's what I thought, too. Well, don't worry about it. It won't come to much. You'll still come out ahead—I told you, my per diem will cover almost all our meal expenses, and——'

'What do you mean, "almost"? You said "all". Val, I don't think you understand, I'm operating on a really tight budget. . .'

'Stop worrying, will you? Living is really cheap here. We'll be fine, you'll see.' Val glanced at her watch. 'Oh, boy, am I in trouble! Barney gave me an hour so I could get you settled in—he'll be foaming at the mouth by now. Look, if you wake up before six, come on down to the set and I'll introduce you around. Anybody can tell you where it is—we're the only action in this God-forsaken place. See you later, OK?'

Danielle sank to the edge of the sofa as soon as the door swung shut. What a disaster this was turning out to be! First the encounter with Lee, now the run-in with Val—and, to top it off, it looked as if her 'free' vacation was going to cost even more than she'd expected.

Sighing, she leaned her head back and stared at the water-stained ceiling. There was always the coward's way out—she could turn tail and head straight back to the States. But it would be awful to try and explain things to Ginny and the others. Besides, her bargain air fare was round-trip; the return ticket was non-refundable and good only on the date it had been issued for, a date some eight weeks from now.

Danielle stood up, then walked slowly across the room to Val's bedroom. She was tired, more tired than she'd realised. What she needed was a nap to clear her head. First, she'd find a space in one of the wardrobes for her empty suitcase, and then she'd take that shower Val had mentioned.

We could climb into a shower together, Lee had said.

Danielle shook her head as she pushed open the bedroom door. Yes, she needed some rest. Definitely.

The room was shadowy. Dark shutters were drawn over the windows, enclosing the room in unnatural twilight. Centred in the midst of the room, sheets rumpled, was a huge four-poster bed.

Slowly, Danielle set down her suitcase. The bed looked almost like a stage set; the linens were white, the canopy lace. Pillows were strewn against the headboard. At the foot, Val's nightgown—black, very sheer—lay in stark relief against the white bedcover.

A hand seemed to close around her throat. 'You can take this sitting-room and I'll keep the bedroom,' Valerie had said, and she had thought only that it was a good idea, a way to keep her cousin's clutter contained.

Now Danielle wondered how she'd been so simple-minded. This bed—Val's bed—wasn't meant for one. This must be where Valerie and Lee Bradford came together. Did his dark head lie on those white pillows, did his golden skin gleam with sweat when. . .?

Her head felt light. Quickly, she slipped from the room and sank down in a chair outside the door. She was trembling. God, what was the matter with her? Val was an adult and so was she. Men and women slept together; it happened all the time. Eddie had teased her about being naïve, but she wasn't ignorant.

After a moment, Danielle rose and made her way to the sofa. She sat down slowly, then drew her legs up and stretched out. A tremor went through her again. I'm cold, she thought, I must be, even on this warm afternoon, and she reached up and drew down the Afghan that lay draped across the back of the sofa.

In a little while, the trembling stopped. Danielle let out a long breath, then closed her eyes. She was exhausted, that was what was wrong with her, it was why all her reactions seemed exaggerated. After a nap, things would look better. Things would look. . .

Her lashes drifted to her cheeks and she slept.

When she awoke, early evening shadows were falling across the walls and floor. Yawning, stretching her arms overhead, Danielle pushed aside the Afghan and swung her legs to the floor. There was a tray on the table in front of the sofa; it held coffee, cream and sugar, along with a plate on which were two croissants and jam. Her stomach growled at the sight.

The coffee was cool, but she drank it thirstily. The croissants were delicious. She ate one, gazed wistfully at the other, then shrugged her shoulders and ate it as well.

She felt a thousand times better when she'd finished. The nap, the food and drink, had restored her spirits and her energy. France, she thought, I'm in France. Smiling, she went to the window and peered out.

The sitting-room overlooked the town square. Below, a black cat crouched in a patch of late sunlight, the tip of its tail twitching gently as it eyed a sparrow. Two old men sat at a scarred wooden table, their heads bent over a backgammon board, their gnarled fingers wrapped loosely around glasses of red wine.

Danielle drew a deep breath. The air was redolent

with the scent of wild flowers and fresh bread. It was, she thought suddenly, a wonderful day to be alive and to be in this place she had for so many years longed to see.

The problems of the morning seemed far simpler now. Money would be tight, but she would manage. She was an old hand at pinching pennies; her parents had left her nothing but loving memories and her aunt and uncle hadn't had any money to spare. If anyone could find a way to get through the summer without going broke, it was she.

As for her relationship with Val—well, she'd known all along she was too old to believe in miracles. Val was Val; she was self-centred, she was selfish—and she still had an eye for the best-looking men.

Poor Val. It was hard not to feel sorry for her. She could say all she wanted about not being jealous, but anyone could see it wasn't true. No matter what she claimed, she didn't like the—what had she called it?—the little game Lee Bradford played with women.

Danielle drew a deep breath. No wonder she'd felt uncomfortable with Lee, right from the start. He hadn't been flirting, he'd been playing a different game. It was one she'd never played, and she wasn't about to start now.

Her smile dimmed. As for Valerie bringing Lee to her bedroom, well, if she did, so be it. This was the twentieth century; Val was entitled to her own code of morality. That was the only reason she was troubled by the thought of Lee and Val together.

It was, wasn't it?

Quickly, before her good mood could slip away, Danielle pulled off her sleep-rumpled clothes and hurried into the bathroom for a quick shower.

* * *

Madame had given her explicit directions to the movie set although Val had been right, she really didn't need them. The town seemed to have accepted the film people calmly enough, but their trucks and trailers took up most of the narrow main street, which led like a compass reading to the fringe of the village where the day's shoot was taking place.

Danielle slowed her steps as she drew closer. She'd expected some sort of glamorous if makeshift film lot. Instead, she saw a tangle of wires and a forest of booms and camera dollies. There were people everywhere, all of them talking a mad mix of French and American-accented English, using words and phrases that were meaningless to her, no matter what the language.

'Heads up!' a voice boomed, and she danced back just in time to keep from being bowled over by two men pushing a giant painting of what looked to be a crowded grandstand. Danielle turned slowly and stared as the picture went by.

'It's called a flat,' a deep voice said softly from just behind her.

Danielle whirled around and found herself looking into the dark blue eyes of Lee Bradford. 'You startled me,' she said.

He smiled lazily. 'I'm glad to see you're fast on your feet. It would be hell to be run down by a grandstand your first day on the set.'

'I thought I'd be out of the way back here,' she said. 'It all looks so confusing.'

Lee nodded. 'It *is* confusing. My first few days, I was convinced it was safer to stand on the track at Le Mans. But it all begins to make a kind of lunatic sense, after a while.' He drew back, looked at her, then smiled. 'Well, for someone who's flown halfway around the world and ended it with a car crash, you don't look half bad.'

He didn't look half bad, either, but she wasn't going

to tell him that. Lee had changed to snug-fitting, faded Levis, a white shirt, open at the throat and rolled to the elbows, and well-worn Nike running shoes. His hair was damp; it glistened with moisture in the setting sun.

He's just come from the shower, she thought, and her hand went, inadvertently, to her hair, still curling wetly against her cheek. Lee's eyes met hers and he laughed softly.

'You see? We could have killed two birds with one stone and saved water to boot.'

Danielle's eyes flashed. 'I wish you wouldn't do that,' she said.

His eyebrows rose. 'Do what? I was only pointing out——'

'What you were doing was teasing me. And I don't like it.'

'Why would you think that?'

Her chin lifted. 'Why do you keep saying things to shock me?'

'Perhaps I'm fascinated by the fact that you shock so easily.'

She looked up at him, gritting her teeth against the laughter she was sure she was to see in his face. But his eyes were scrious. The realisation set her off balance, and she felt a flush rise to her cheeks.

'How do you do that, Danielle?'

She blinked. 'How do I. . .?'

'Blush, I mean. It's lovely.'

'It's not lovely at all,' she said irritably. 'It just seems to be something that—that. . .'

'That happens when you're with me?' A smile tilted across his mouth. 'I'd like to think that was true.'

'Why? Because it amuses you?'

'No.' His eyes swept over her face, lingering at her mouth before meeting hers again. 'It doesn't amuse me at all.'

Danielle drew a deep breath. Games, she thought, remembering, he plays games, and somehow he was drawing her into this one. But he couldn't, not if she refused to play.

'Perhaps I'll see you around,' she said evenly. 'Good afternoon, Mr Bradford.'

'Lee,' he said, falling in beside her as she began walking towards the set. 'I thought we settled that.'

'Lee, then. I wish you'd just——'

'Would you like to take a look around?'

She shook her head. 'No, thank you. I'll wait for Val.'

'Val's holed up with Wexler. By the time she shows again, it's liable to be tomorrow.' His hand closed lightly but firmly on her elbow. 'Come on, I'll walk you through.'

Her skin tingled where his fingers touched it, as if there were a low current of electricity flowing between them.

'That's all right,' she said, pulling away from him. 'I don't mind waiting.'

'Look, you almost got run down a few minutes ago. Don't you think you'd better have some idea of what things are before you go wandering off and get into trouble.?'

He was right; there was equipment stacked everywhere. She nodded reluctantly.

'I suppose.'

Lee smiled. 'That's better. After all, you want to make a good first impression.'

Danielle looked at him. 'Yes, but on whom? I've never seen so many people jammed into one place. Do they all really belong here?'

He grinned at her. 'You'd better believe it. Watch it,' he said. His arm slipped around her shoulders and he steered her past a snarl of cables that lay curled like black snakes at their feet.

She laughed nervously. 'I guess I'd better learn to watch where I walk.'

'You'll get used to it after a few days.' He glanced down at her and smiled. 'So, what do you think?'

His arm was still around her, his hand lightly cupping her shoulder. The same tingle as before raced along her spine.

'It—it's confusing.'

'Very.' Lee smiled again. 'Especially to an outsider.'

'I'll learn,' she said defensively.

He laughed. 'I'm sure you will. But I wasn't referring to you; I was talking about myself.'

She looked up at him in surprise. 'You? But you're not——'

'Ah, but I am. This is a strange world to me, Danielle. I'm used to cars and engines—things you can touch and make sense of. This,' he said, gesturing with his free hand, 'is a place of illusion. Nothing's quite as it seems here.'

No, she thought suddenly, nothing was. Take Lee Bradford, for example. A little while ago, he'd been the last man on earth she'd wanted to see again. Now, here they were, walking along together, chatting comfortably with each other. Val would be surprised. Val would. . .

Val.

'Where did you say Val was?' she asked quickly. 'In Mr Wexler's office?'

'Probably.'

'Why don't we walk over there, then?'

Lee grinned. 'Barney hates to be disturbed when he's working. Don't worry about it; Val takes care of herself.'

'Val's job must be interesting.'

'It would be more interesting if she understood more than two or three words of French,' he said mildly.

Danielle nodded. 'Val says——'

Lee drew to a halt. 'All right,' he said, turning her towards him, 'what's going on?'

'I don't know what you——'

'Yes, you do. You've managed to mention your cousin's name every second breath. I assume there's a reason.'

Danielle looked at him. 'I should think you'd be mentioning her name yourself,' she said quietly. 'After all, you and she. . .'

Lee let go of her and stuffed his hands into the back pockets of his jeans. His eyes darkened dangerously. 'Go on,' he said softly. 'What did she tell you?'

'Everything,' she said, lifting her chin.

He smiled tightly. 'Somehow,' he said softly, 'I doubt that.'

His tone mocked her, but she held her ground. 'There's no point to this, you know,' she said quietly. 'I mean, I think Val's a fool to put up with it, but if she's satisfied——'

'There you are, Danni.' Danielle looked up at the sound of Valerie's voice. Her cousin was smiling, but her tone was frigid. 'I was beginning to wonder if you'd decided to sleep the day away.'

'I awoke a little while ago. I came looking for you, and Mr Bradford——'

'Lee,' he said pleasantly. 'I thought we settled that in Nice.' He smiled at Valerie, but his eyes were cool. 'I didn't think Danielle should be on her own her first day.'

'Aren't you sweet, Lee?' Val said, smiling blithely at him. She linked her arm through his. 'It was good of you to take my little cousin under your wing. Has she asked dozens of silly questions?'

Lee looked at Danielle, and his smile warmed. 'One or two.'

'Well, I'll take over now—although there won't be much to see, everybody seems to have finished for the day. I wonder, Danni, would you mind terribly if we put off our tour until tomorrow?'

'No,' Danielle said quickly, 'no, that would be fine.'

Val pursed her lips. 'Actually,' she said thoughtfully, 'you look rather tired. Don't you think she looks tired, Lee?'

His teeth glinted in a quick smile. 'I think she looks just fine.'

There was a pause and then Danielle cleared her throat. 'I—I do feel rather tired, now that I think about it. Would you mind very much if I went back to the inn, Val?'

This time, Valerie's smile was genuine. 'No, of course not. I understand. What you probably need is a good hot meal and then a solid night's rest. Why don't you ask Madame to fix you something, hmm? She makes an awfully good omelette.' She looked up at Lee as she moved closer to him. Her fingers curled more closely around his arm. 'Some of the crew is driving into Nice for dinner. I told them I'd round you up and we'd join them.'

'Sounds good,' Lee said. 'But I'm afraid I can't make it tonight. I have an early-morning meeting with the stunt co-ordinator.'

Val pouted prettily. 'Don't be silly, Lee. You have to have dinner somewhere.'

He smiled as he gently took her hand from his arm. 'Yeah, that's true.' His eyes met Danielle's. 'Maybe I'll try one of Madame's omelettes—if Danielle doesn't mind having company.'

In the abrupt silence, the only sound Danielle could hear was the rasp of her own breath. The man was incorrigible, she thought. How could he behave like this?

Val tossed back her cloud of platinum hair. 'Well,' she said briskly, 'I can see I'm outvoted.' A bright smile blazed across her face. 'So I'll make it easy for all of us.

I'll settle for an omelette, too.' Her eyes, glinting like icy green shards, met Danielle's. 'How does that sound?'

Danielle swallowed drily. 'It sounds—it sounds. . .'

Later, lying sleepless on the lumpy sofa-bed mattress, she would remember that moment and wonder if she'd have ever managed an answer. As it was, Lee stepped in and rescued her.

'Terrific,' he said, and he draped his arms lightly around both women's shoulders. 'After all, we can't leave Danielle alone her first night in France, can we, Val?'

Time seemed to stop while Val stared past Lee to Danielle.

'So it would seem,' she said finally, and the coldness in her voice made a mockery of her brightly glittering smile.

CHAPTER FIVE

THE door to the Wexler offices flew open and slammed loudly against the wall, propelled as much by an impatient assistant as by the hot Provençal breeze. Danielle looked up as the memo she'd been reading sailed off her desk.

The man scooped up the paper in mid-air and handed it to her. 'Sorry,' he said with an apologetic smile. 'Mr Wexler says if you could just take care of this one last thing?'

Barney Wexler's cramped handwriting angled across the slip of paper. Danielle read it quickly, then nodded.

'No problem.'

The man grimaced as he pushed the door open again. 'Jeez, it's so hot! I can't wait until we're outta here and back in the real world.'

Danielle sighed as the door closed, and then she swivelled her chair towards the window behind her and stared out into the street.

He was right, she thought, this timeless village wasn't the real world. But she'd come to love its charm in just a few days.

Val thought she was crazy. Ste Agathe was too 'foreign'. The food, the people, the old houses were not for her, she said with distaste. Even the smoky café, Le Lapin Gris, where the crew gathered over bottles of *vin ordinaire* at day's end, couldn't please her.

'Dull,' Val said, 'dull, dull, *dull*!'

Quiet, Danielle thought, quiet, peaceful, ageless.

But all that would change after this weekend. Not the

village—it would go on as it always had, even after the Wexler company had taken down its sets and moved on.

No, the change would come because Lee would be back late tonight. And who knew what would happen then?

The memory of that first awful evening was still sharply etched in her mind. The dining-room at the *auberge* had been closed. Danielle had breathed a sigh of relief, thinking she'd been granted a reprieve. But Lee had insisted on going to Le Lapin Gris, where the three of them had crowded around a small table. The chairs had been rickety and close together; Lee's thigh had pressed against hers once and she'd pulled her leg back as if from a fire.

But Lee hadn't seem to notice. He'd kept the conversation going despite Val's silence and hers, asking her questions about herself that she'd answered in monosyllables. After a while, Val had tried to divert him by telling gossipy stories about the film's famous star and his latest girlfriend, but finally she'd fallen silent. A little while later, she'd made an impatient sound and said it was awfully late and Danielle looked exhausted, and why didn't they walk her to the inn so she could get some rest?

It was cool outside, surprisingly so after the unremitting heat of the day. Danielle had shivered in her light cotton top and trousers.

Lee glanced at her. 'Are you cold?' Before she could answer, he slipped off his denim jacket and draped it around her shoulders. His hand brushed against her cheek. 'Is that better?'

No, she thought, not better at all. The jacket smelled of him, it carried the heat of his body, and she had a sudden desire to turn her face towards the soft collar and burrow into it.

'Yes,' she said in a tight voice.

'Good,' he said, smiling at her. 'We don't want you to come down with pneumonia your first night here, do we, Val?'

Val glared across him. 'No,' she said through her teeth. 'Of course we don't.'

They walked in silence to the dark *auberge*. As soon as they reached it, Danielle moved ahead.

'Goodnight,' she called as she fled up the steps. Safe in Val's rooms, she closed the door and leaned back against it. Her legs were trembling, as if she'd run a race.

What was happening to her? She already knew all she needed to know about Lee Bradford: he had no morals and no conscience. But that didn't keep her from—from acting like a fool when he. . .

She was still wearing his jacket. Her breath caught. Slowly, her hand lifted to the denim, her fingers moved lightly across it, and then she did what she'd almost done when Lee had draped his jacket over her shoulders, she did what she couldn't keep herself from doing—she pulled it off, lifted it to her face, and closed her eyes.

She stood that way for a long time. When finally she heard the sound of Val's footsteps tapping up the stairs, her eyes flew open and she flung the jacket from her, hating Lee, cursing herself, wondering if any of what was happening would ever make any kind of sense.

She looked up when the door opened, praying Val would let the insanity of the evening die a quiet death. But her cousin was taut with barely suppressed rage. Her pretty face was drawn into a series of thin, down-slashing lines.

'What the hell are you trying to do?' she spat.

For a moment, Danielle thought of pretending she didn't know what Val was talking about. But there wasn't much sense to that. She wasn't a fool, and neither was Val.

'I'm not trying to do anything,' she said. 'It's he who——'

Her cousin's mouth twisted. 'I told you how he is, Danni. If you lead him on——'

'For God's sake, Val, face the facts. Don't blame this on me.'

'Oh, come on, Danni, I wasn't born yesterday!' Val kicked off her high-heeled shoes, then stalked across the room. 'All that blushing, those coy little looks from beneath your lashes. . .' She stopped at the bedroom door and stared at Danielle. 'What will you do if he tries to take you up on your invitation, hmm?' Her eyes were cold. 'Lee's a man, Danni, not a boy. He's not your Teddy or Eddie or whoever it was you kept dangling.'

'I didn't "dangle" him, Val—you don't know what you're talking about. As for Lee Bradford, I keep telling you, I'm not the least bit interested. Frankly, I don't know what you find so fascinating about him. He's a—an egotistical, smug bastard, and I. . .'

Val's eyes flashed. 'And you want him, the same as every other woman does.' Colour swept to Danielle's cheeks and Val gave a harsh laugh. 'You can't even deny it, can you?'

'I don't like him, Val. I told you. . .'

Val smiled unpleasantly. 'Liking him hasn't a thing to do with it. We're not talking about sugar-coated emotions here, we're talking about something far more basic, Miss Innocent. We're talking about sex. Or is that too raw a topic for my little Missouri cousin?'

The two women stared at each other, and then Danielle let out her breath.

'Coming here was a mistake,' she said softly. 'I knew it all along.'

Val tossed her head. 'I couldn't agree more,' she said, and then she yanked open the door to the bedroom and slammed it after her.

Angry tears rose in Danielle's eyes and she brushed them away with a quick swipe of her hand. Coming here had been more than a mistake—it had been stupid. She didn't belong here—Lee had said this was a strange world, but it was more than that. It was alien, a place where people played at things she didn't understand.

First thing tomorrow morning, she'd pack her things and get out.

Resolutely, she undressed, put on her nightgown, and opened the sofa-bed. As she reached for the light switch, she saw Lee's jacket lying in a heap on the floor and she bent towards it, hesitating at the last moment as if picking it up might burn her hand.

What nonsense, she thought, snatching it up and tossing it aside. She climbed between the rough muslin sheets and lay on her back, glaring up at the moonlight-dappled ceiling. It was only a jacket, and Lee was only a man who got his kicks out of playing with women. And she, fool that she was, had made the game easy.

Little girl, he'd called her, little farm girl, and she'd been quick to tell him she was neither. Danielle gritted her teeth as she rolled over and punched her pillow into shape. He was probably still laughing at that one—he could fluster her with a glance, and he knew it.

And now she was going to turn and run. The thought was humiliating, but what else could she do? It wasn't worth staying and facing him down—was it?

Maybe it was. There was her pride to consider. And there was the cost of a ticket home. You couldn't measure pride in dollars, but you could certainly measure how far into the hole she'd be once she paid for it. She had expenses waiting back home, a car that had long needed costly repairs, a living-room that was in desperate need of decent furniture.

Damn Lee Bradford! She wasn't going to go into debt because of him. Danielle pulled the blanket up and closed her eyes. She was done being a game-piece, and tomorrow he'd find that out.

She awakened with a throbbing in her head and an ache in her back. Bright sunlight filled the shabby room.

'Good morning.'

Val's voice startled her. Her cousin was sitting in one of the overstuffed armchairs, smiling, holding a cup of milky coffee in her outstretched hand.

Danielle pushed a tangle of brown curls back from her face. 'Good morning,' she said with a cautious smile. 'Is that for me?'

'It's a peace offering. I'm afraid we got off to a bad start last night.'

Danielle took the cup from her. 'Val——'

'No. Don't say anything, Danni. Let me talk, please.' Her cousin looked at her. 'Do you think you could just forget everything I said? I don't know what got into me—I guess maybe I've been working too hard or something.'

'Val, please. I——'

'I'd be very grateful if you'd give it another try.'

Danielle looked at her. She wanted to believe Val's little speech, wanted to believe the look of innocence on her face. But things had gone too far for that, and she smiled gently as she pushed the blankets aside.

'It's all right,' she said, swinging her legs to the floor. 'I'm not going to leave you in the lurch, Val. We made an agreement, and I'll stick to my end of it.' She reached for her robe, then stood up. 'Your boyfriend bowled me over,' she said calmly. 'I'm not used to sharks like him.' Her eyes met Val's. 'And you were right, in a way. It's my fault he's been after me. Oh, I don't mean that I've been leading him on—it's just that he knows he can get a rise out of me, and that seems to amuse him.' She lifted her chin. 'Well, that's finished.'

Valerie stared at her. 'Is it?' Her voice had lost all its warmth.

Danielle's gaze fell on Lee's jacket and her throat tightened. 'Yes. Believe me, you needn't be concerned any longer.'

Val's eyebrows rose. 'I was annoyed, Danni, but never concerned.' She smiled thinly. 'Anyway, all this is academic. You see, Lee's gone.'

Danielle stared at her cousin. 'Gone?'

'Well, until the end of the week, anyway. Something came up, I didn't pay attention to the details. I think it had to do with his racing team or his car—whatever, he left this morning and he won't be back until late Friday evening.'

Danielle turned away and let out her breath. 'That—that's good,' she said softly.

It was, wasn't it?

Val glanced at her watch and made a face. 'Goodness, just look at the time. Barney—Mr Wexler—will have my head! Let's get moving.'

The production company offices were housed in a battered aluminium caravan parked on a dusty street. Danielle entered hesitantly, expecting a jumble of tight little rooms. But the caravan proved to be relatively spacious, with most of the interior walls gone. The floor space was given over to a scattering of file cabinets and office furniture. There were typewriters and computers, all humming, thanks to the portable generator outside.

Barney Wexler was a rumpled-looking, paunchy man with a shiny bald head. He looked up from his desk when the women entered. 'Well, well,' he said, squinting over a pair of half-frame reading glasses, 'the little Missouri cousin, at last.'

Wexler was smiling. But on this morning the phrase was like a gauntlet tossed at Danielle's feet.

'Well, well,' she said coolly, 'the big Hollywood producer, at last.'

There was a thunderous silence, and then Val made a sound that was half-gasp, half-laugh. 'Danni! Good lord. . .Barney—Mr Wexler—I'm sorry. I don't know what got into——'

The bray of Wexler's laughter cut short Val's apology. 'I apologise,' he said, getting to his feet and offering Danielle his hand. 'I expected someone quite different.'

Danielle smiled. 'Someone with hay in her hair?'

Wexler glanced at Val. 'Something like that,' he said, and then he motioned her to a chair beside his desk. 'Val, bring us some coffee. Unless you'd prefer something cold?'

'Coffee's fine,' Danielle said quickly. 'But Val doesn't have to——'

'She might as well do something,' Wexler said blandly. 'Now, sit down, Miss Nichols, and tell me why you let your cousin talk you into saving her skin.'

An hour later, after she'd translated a handful of memos and fielded an irate call from the mayor of Ste Agathe, Wexler had smiled and told her he was putting her on the payroll.

'Per diem, of course,' he'd added quickly.

'Of course,' Danielle had agreed, and she'd smiled gratefully.

Now, only a few days later, she'd settled into what had become a comfortable routine. She rose early, before Val stirred, and spent an hour or two in the makeshift office, dealing with whatever had come up the previous day. By mid-morning she was on the road, tooling along in the ancient Citröen that Madame had arranged for her to rent from her brother, the butcher.

The car guzzled precious petrol with frightening greed and had a disconcerting habit of getting stuck in gear. But it was the only car available for hire in Ste Agathe, and it cost half what Danielle would have paid at a car rental agency in Nice.

Once she'd got used to its eccentricities, the car proved dependable. So far, it had taken her to the Musée Chagall in Nice, the Roman ruins at Cimiez, and the beautiful stands of pine at Cap d'Antibes. She'd changed her routine today, coming back in the late afternoon to put in an hour's work because she was going to be gone all weekend. She was going to Cannes.

The decision had been a sudden one, made just that morning.

'Lee's coming back tonight,' Val had said while Danielle had been rummaging in her drawer for a scarf. 'We'll probably have dinner out, but afterwards. . .' The ensuing pause had been long and deliberate. 'It won't bother you if we come back here, will it, Danni? You're not going to be upset or anything like that?'

Danielle had fought against the nausea that rose in her throat. 'No,' she'd said finally. 'In fact—in fact, I won't be here. I'm driving to Cannes and I thought—I thought I'd stay the weekend.'

'What a wonderful idea,' Val had said quickly.

And it was a wonderful idea, Danielle thought now, looking out into the street. Cannes would be fun, the guidebooks said so. Then why wasn't she excited about going? Why wasn't she looking forward to——?

'Danni?' She blinked and looked up. Barney Wexler was watching her from the open doorway.

'Mr Wexler.' She pushed back her chair and got to her feet. 'I was just finishing up. The notice for the lighting crew is——'

Wexler smiled. 'Yes, yes. I'm sure it's all taken care of. I came to tell you we're running the car gag soon. Don't you want to see it?'

'The car gag?'

Wexler nodded. 'Believe me, if you've never seen a

gag, this is the one to start with. Billy and Chico swear nothing like it has been done before.'

Danielle shook her head. 'What's a car gag? Is it a joke of some kind?'

Wexler grinned. 'A joke—that's good, Danni. Chico will——' Someone called his name and he waved impatiently. 'OK, hold your horses!' he yelled, and then he looked at her again. 'I know you're in a rush, but do yourself a favour and watch this thing. If they pull it off, it oughtta be terrific.'

His footsteps clattered down the steps as the door swung shut after him. Danielle walked to the window and peered out. Twilight was falling; the village lay in amethyst shadows. Just ahead, where the street became a narrow road leading into the mountains, a small crowd was gathering. She could see a forest of camera and mike booms. After a moment, she shrugged her shoulders and walked to the door.

Why not? she thought. A car gag, whatever that was, might be interesting, although how you could film a joke about a car was beyond her. This film, or what little she knew of it, was about a Frenchman, a Grand Prix driver. It was the story of his life, told in flashback, from the little village of his birth to his eventual victories on the international racing circuit.

Nothing about that sounded terribly funny. Still, you could never tell with movie-making. The little time she'd spent on the perimeters of the set had told her that.

Standing on tiptoe on the fringe of the crowd, Danielle could just make out the scene. It had grown darker now; the cameras would be filming under Klieg lights. They were set up to shoot the road from different angles, some on dollies, some hand-held. The road itself glistened like a dark ribbon, and Danielle was puzzled for a moment until she saw the huge tank-truck parked nearby.

'Soak it down again!' a voice yelled. 'I want it to look as if it's just rained cats and dogs.'

The truck moved in and water poured over the road. Danielle felt a little catch in her throat.

A picture sprang into her mind. Water, gleaming darkly on a wet road. . .

'You ready, Al?' somebody yelled.

A man appeared from the crowd of make-up people and technicians. 'Yeah,' he said. He walked slowly towards the shoulder of the road.

'Billy? Is Chico all set?'

Someone wearing headphones and carrying a small radio raised his hand and waved it.

'OK, tell him we're gonna roll. And tell him to remember to hit those brakes when he comes around that curve. I want burning rubber, man, as much as he can deliver. When this gag rolls, everybody in the theatre's gonna wet their pants!'

There was a murmur of nervous laughter. 'Quiet on the set!' a voice called. There was silence, and then someone yelled, 'Action!' Far in the distance, there was the sudden, ominous roar of an engine.

The car was only a dark speck at first, racing towards the cameras from the mountains. But it was going fast, terribly fast, rocketing from side to side as it drew nearer. It skidded around the first curve, leaning over until it was almost riding on only two wheels, and the assembled onlookers seemed to draw in their collective breath.

Her mind skittered back in time to a different wet road, to a car travelling too fast, faster than it should, skidding as it came around the corner. . .

Danielle's throat went dry. She looked frantically towards the actor walking slowly along the shoulder, head down, hands tucked into his pockets, then to the car racing wildly down the road.

No, she thought, no one would do this deliberately, no one would. . .

'Eddie!' she screamed, but it was too late. Her cry was lost in the tortured squeal of rubber as the car skidded across the wet road, and then it was on the walking man, he was rising into the air, turning, turning, turning. . .

She was sobbing softly when strong arms closed tightly around her.

'It's all right,' a husky voice whispered, 'it's OK.'

'Help him,' she said brokenly, 'please, help him. He's dying.'

'Danielle. Shh, baby, it's all right, I promise.'

The arms that held her tightened as she began to tremble, then swung her off her feet.

'Please,' she whispered, 'oh, please, don't let him die.'

'No one's going to die,' the voice said. 'It wasn't real, Danielle. It was a stunt.'

A stunt. It was a stunt. The world reeled around her as the man carried her away from the stench of burning rubber and tortured metal.

Slowly, the planet righted itself. Eddie hadn't died again. No one had. What she'd seen had just been a trick, a film-maker's illusion.

But the arms that enfolded her, this heart that beat so steadily beneath her ear, this voice that whispered reassurances—all of that was real. And all of it belonged to Lee Bradford, whose long strides had taken them quickly from the crowded set.

Danielle drew a shaky breath. 'I—I'm all right now,' she said. 'You can put me down.'

Lee's arms tightened around her. 'In a minute.'

'Lee, please, put me down. I feel like such a fool.'

'Why? Because you couldn't tell the real thing from the gag?' He laughed softly. 'Chico would be happy to hear it.'

'A gag,' she said, shuddering, 'that's what Barney said it was. But it wasn't, it was. . .'

'Here we go.' Lee let her down slowly, and she saw

that he'd brought her to his car. His arm stayed around her as he opened the door. 'Come on, get in.' When she hesitated, he smiled. 'No gags, I promise. Just a nice, quiet drive to a nice, quiet spot where you can get your bearings. OK?'

'Thank you. But. . .'

'But what?'

She stared at him. But I hate you, she wanted to say. And I'm not going to let you make a fool of me any more.

But the words wouldn't come. Lee was watching her with a half-smile on his mouth, his eyes dark as they swept across her face. I missed you, she thought suddenly, and the realisation sent another wave of dizziness through her.

Lee cursed softly as she stumbled back against him. 'Come on,' he said, pulling open the car door, 'get in.'

'No. I can't. I. . .'

A ragged cheer drifted towards them on the warm air, and Lee looked up.

'They're celebrating,' he said. 'The gag went well and it's Friday night. That means the crew's going to knock off and spend the next few hours talking about what a terrific crash it was.' He smiled tightly. 'Is that what you want to do?'

Danielle shook her head. 'I was going to drive to Cannes,' she said, and then she looked out into the darkness gathering over the mountains and she shuddered. 'But not now.'

She let him hand her into the car. He closed the door after her, then came around to the driver's side and got in.

'We'll have a drink, relax, have an early dinner—and then I'll bring you back, safe and sound. All right?'

She knew there were a dozen reasons to say no, but at that moment none of them seemed to matter. Lee took her silence as agreement. He turned the key, put his foot to the accelerator, and the car swung away from the kerb.

'Lee.' Danielle took a deep breath as she remembered her cousin's preparations for the evening. 'Val's expecting you.'

The car slipped into the darkening night. 'Is she?' he said carelessly. He glanced at her, then looked back at the road. 'What happened back there?'

Danielle shook her head. She didn't want to talk about it, not now, not with the images of the crash that had killed Eddie so fresh in her mind.

'I—I guess I just got carried away. It all seemed so real.' She smiled shakily. 'Do they really call a thing like that a gag?'

Lee's teeth flashed in the growing darkness. 'Crazy, huh?' His foot eased on the accelerator as he swung the car on to a crossroads. Lights gleamed ahead.

'Noble,' he said, and he laughed softly. 'Even smaller than Ste Agathe, if you can imagine that.' He signalled a right turn, then pulled off the road beside a small, lighted house. A wooden sign creaked in the wind. La Salamandre, it read.

Lee shut off the engine. Silence fell around them, broken by the whirr of crickets.

'What is this place?' Danielle asked after a moment.

'An inn. A pretty good one—I had dinner here a couple of times.' Leather creaked as he shifted towards her. 'Are you sure you're all right now?'

She nodded. 'Yes, I'm fine. I just—I feel so dumb.'

He shook his head. 'You're not,' he said softly. He smiled as he reached out and stroked a curl back from her cheek. 'I missed you.'

Her heart turned over. 'Don't be silly,' she said quickly. 'I—I didn't even realise you were gone.'

Leather creaked again as he moved closer to her. 'Danielle.'

His voice was low. It sent a tremor along her skin.

'Lee,' she said, and she swallowed drily. 'You said—you said something about a drink and dinner.'

'Danielle. Look at me.'

'No.' Her voice was a whisper. 'I—I've changed my mind. I want to go back to Ste Agathe.'

'Look at me,' he insisted.

His hand closed on her chin and slowly, inexorably, he lifted her face to his. It was very dark now; only the faint light from the inn illuminated his face.

'Please,' she whispered. 'Take me back.'

'You know that's not what you want.'

Oh, God, she thought, what was happening? She knew what kind of man he was, she knew this was all a game to him. But his breath was warm against her face, his hand strong yet strangely gentle. And the air between them was charged, just as it had been that other time they'd sat close together in this little oasis, when she'd felt as if she and Lee Bradford were the only people in the world.

A tingle of warning raced along her spine. 'Don't,' she whispered. Lee's hand moved to the back of her head and cupped it, his fingers tangling in the cascade of her hair.

'Why do women say "don't" when they mean "do"?' he said softly.

The tingle grew stronger. 'Please, Lee. This is wrong. I don't want you to. . .'

'Come here,' he whispered, drawing her to him. 'That's it. Just relax. Just. . .'

His mouth brushed hers, lightly at first, then harder. She caught her breath as his other arm went around her.

'Danielle,' he said, 'Danielle—I thought about this all week, about kissing you and touching you. . .'

She gasped as his hand slid to just below her breast. His fingers moved lightly, gently, the tip of his thumb grazing her nipple as it drifted over her thin cotton shirt.

'Don't,' she said again, 'Lee, please don't.'

Her eyes shut as his hand moved on her again. All the sensations she'd ever imagined were passing from his touch to her flesh; she could feel her nipple tightening, budding against his questing fingers.

Lights danced behind her closed lids. Lee, she thought, Lee. . .

'Yes,' he murmured, and she realised she'd somehow said his name aloud. 'Yes,' he said again, as her hand lifted and spread on his chest.

He groaned as his mouth dropped to hers. His kiss almost stopped her heart. She felt herself heating, opening, like the seed of some primordial plant that needed fire to flower.

'Lee,' she sighed, and her hands moved up his chest to his face, moved across his features as if she were blind and needed her hands to see. She whispered his name again, and then she wound her arms around his neck and raised herself to him.

Lee murmured something. Suddenly, his hands bit into her arms. She heard the rasp of his breath, and then he put her from him.

Her eyes opened slowly. 'Lee?' she whispered.

In the faint light from the inn, she could see only his eyes. They were dark, almost black, glittering with an emotion she couldn't define. A muscle knotted in his cheek.

'Get out of the car,' he said.

Danielle drew in her breath. 'What?'

His face twisted. 'Get out, damn you!' He reached past her and shoved her door open. 'Did you hear me, Danielle? I said. . .'

The look in his eyes, the anger in his voice, terrified

her. Had he done this to humiliate her? No, she thought, no.

'Get out!'

She stumbled out of the door, almost falling to her knees in her hurry to get away. Lee stared at her.

'There's a phone inside.' His voice was sharp. 'Call Wexler and ask him to send a car for you. Do you understand?'

She shook her head as she backed slowly away. 'No,' she whispered, 'I don't understand. You—you can't have done this just to—just to. . .'

He laughed then, a terrible, raw sound that Danielle knew she would remember for the rest of her life.

'You're right,' he said, 'you *don't* understand, not one damned bit, and that's the trouble.'

He pulled the door closed and it slammed loudly, and then the engine roared to life and the car shot on to the road.

Later, she would remember that eye witnesses to tragedies always said things seemed to happen in slow motion. But it wasn't so; everything that came next happened with terrible speed.

There was a curve just beyond the inn. The car reached it just as an old tractor, emerging from a hidden road, suddenly appeared in its headlights. The horrible sound of tyres grasping desperately at the road's surface echoed in the night, and the headlights began to swing in erratic arcs as the car veered sharply towards the precipice that flanked the narrow road.

For a heart-stopping instant, it seemed to hang delicately on the edge, the headlights waving an urgent plea, and then slowly, almost primly, the car toppled and vanished into the dark.

CHAPTER SIX

DANIELLE swallowed the last of her coffee, crumpled the paper cup, and tossed it into the waste bin. The sound was unnaturally loud in the early-morning silence of the hospital waiting-room and she looked quickly at Valerie, who lay curled on a peeling vinyl sofa.

But her cousin slept on, undisturbed, and Danielle breathed a sigh of relief. The last thing she wanted was to have to deal with Val's hysteria again.

'They're giving him blood?' Val had shrieked when the emergency-room nurse had offered an update on Lee's condition. 'I don't want to hear about it. I'll faint, I know I will!'

And when the orthopaedist had appeared to explain that the fracture in Lee's right ankle would require a steel plate and pins, she'd slumped into a chair and lowered her head to her knees.

'Please,' she'd whispered, 'spare me the details.'

Danielle had followed the doctor into the hall, eager for the 'details'. They were proof that Lee was alive, that he hadn't died the way Eddie had.

The accident had brought back all the memories of that terrible evening.

She was supposed to have met Eddie at six, but she'd been late. And not even for a very good reason—she'd been late because she'd stood around talking with her students after the French Club meeting instead of hurrying to keep her date. That was why Eddie had been standing on the pavement outside the restaurant when a car had come around the corner too fast on the rain-slicked road and. . .

Eddie had been dead when she'd reached him. Lee, thank God, had been alive. She had no idea how she'd got to him: one minute, she had been on the road and the next, she had been on the steep slope of the embankment, cradling Lee in her arms, begging him not to die, even though she'd known he couldn't hear her.

Lee had been unconscious, his dark lashes lying like soot against his cheeks, blood welling across his temple, dark crimson against the unnatural pallor of his skin. And his foot had been bent at an angle so impossible that she'd felt a sudden clench of nausea in her belly.

But none of that had been as important as the steady rise and fall of his chest. He was alive. Alive! Danielle had laughed through her tears and bent her head to his, whispering her joy to him, as if he could, by some miracle, hear her.

She'd refused to give him up to the ambulance attendants.

'You can ride with him,' one said finally, his French so thick with the accent of Provence that at first she misundestood. In desperation, the man finally threw his hands to the sky and motioned her to the rear of the ambulance, and she nodded and climbed inside.

When they reached the hospital, the emergency-room nurse had to ease her from Lee's side.

'You must let the doctors do their work,' she said softly, putting her arm around Danielle's shoulders.

She stared at the woman, her expression fierce. 'He has to live,' she said. 'Do you understand?'

'I will bring coffee to you in the waiting-room, *mademoiselle*. Perhaps you wish to notify someone of the gentleman's accident?'

Danielle stared at her. 'I—I don't know. . .' Val, she thought suddenly, and she nodded. 'There is someone. I suppose I should. . .'

Val arrived in a breathless rush. 'Danni, how is he?'

'He's alive, that's all I know.' Danielle's eyes filled with tears. 'I saw it happen.'

Valerie stared at her. 'You saw it? I don't understand.'

Danielle bowed her head. 'He—he noticed me watching the crash this afternoon—the stunt, you know, the one on the set. I—I got upset; it reminded me of——'

'Get to the point,' Val snapped.

'We drove to Noble. And Lee parked outside an *auberge*. We talked, and then—and then. . .'

Valerie's breath hissed. 'And then?' she prompted.

Danielle's face lifted slowly to the other woman's. Val was watching her through eyes gone cold and dead.

Dear God in heaven! What was she saying? She couldn't tell Valerie what had happened—that Lee had tried to make love to her, that she'd melted in his arms, that somehow her compliance had angered him or repelled him so much that he'd driven off in a rage and—and. . .

'Well? I'm waiting, Danni. What happened?'

Danielle drew in her breath. 'I—I decided I wanted to go back to Ste Agathe,' she said, the evasive answer bitter on her tongue. 'Lee said he was going to drive on. I got out of the car and. . .'

But Valerie had stopped listening. 'Your dress,' she said. 'It's covered with blood. Why didn't you ask me to bring you a change of clothing?'

Danielle had glanced down at herself in surprise. 'I—I didn't realise. . .'

Her cousin had shuddered delicately. 'The sight of blood makes me ill.'

As it turned out, so had the mention of surgery or broken bones. It had been a relief when Valerie had finally curled into a corner of the waiting-room sofa.

'Wake me when there's news.' She'd yawned, and promptly fallen into a deep sleep.

Now, hours later, Danielle watched Val's peaceful

face and wondered how she could sleep while Lee—while Lee. . .

Quickly, she walked to the window and stared out. Dawn was just breaking over Nice; streets that would soon be crowded with tourists stretched, deserted, towards the sea. She could see no one except a man and woman, still in party clothes, slowly strolling arm in arm, wishing the hours of the night never to end.

But that was impossible. Time was a river; there was no way to stop its flow. Oh, but if only you could! Closing her eyes, Danielle pressed her forehead to the cool glass. How wonderful it would be to go back to this afternoon and wipe the slate clean, erase everything that had brought Lee to that terrible moment when his car had skidded off the road.

'Mademoiselle Nichols?'

She spun towards the doorway. A man in green sterile clothes smiled wearily as he walked into the room.

Danielle stepped forward. 'Yes?'

'I am Dr Bonet,' he said, holding out his hand. 'I am—how do you say?—a surgeon of orthopaedics, *n'est-ce pas*?'

'Yes,' she said again. Stupid, she thought. Ask him how Lee is. Ask him if he's all right.' 'Yes,' she whispered, clasping his hand and looking into his face, letting her eyes ask all the questions there were.

Dr Bonet cleared his throat. 'Monsieur Bradford is a very strong man, *mademoiselle*. He is in excellent health.'

'Is he?' What was he saying? Lee was lying somewhere inside this hospital, his leg broken, his face bleeding. . .

The doctor smiled gently. 'What I mean to say is that it is good that he is in such fine condition, do you understand? It gives him the strength he needs now, to withstand the trauma he has suffered.'

Danielle drew a ragged breath. 'Dr Bonet, please—how is he? Is he. . .is he. . .?'

The vinyl sofa creaked as Valerie rose to her feet. 'What she's trying to ask,' she said in an impatient, sleep-roughened voice, 'is whether Lee's in one piece.' Her heels tapped as she crossed the floor towards them. 'Well? Is he?'

'His leg, as you know, is broken at the ankle. And he has torn the medial collateral ligament—he has sustained damage to his knee.'

'But he'll be all right?' Danielle's voice trembled.

'He has come through the worst of it—the surgery, the loss of blood—quite well.' Bonet paused, then pursed his lips. 'The knee is a difficult injury to treat. As for the ankle. . .' He shook his head. 'There was much shattered bone. The joint——'

Val held up her hand. 'But you fixed all that, right? What about his face? My cousin said there was a gash. Is it bad?'

'We took some stitches.'

'How does he look?' Val said quickly. 'Will he need plastic surgery?'

The doctor's eyebrows rose. 'No, I think not. There may be a scar, but not a serious one.' He paused and looked from one woman to the other.

Danielle wet her lips. 'Then—then he's going to be all right?'

Bonet looked at her. 'None of his injuries are life-threatening, *mademoiselle*.'

The words, so quietly spoken, brought tears of happiness to her eyes.

'Thank you,' she whispered, and she laughed softly as she brushed the back of her hand across her lashes. 'Thank you so much, Doctor.'

'We have only done what we could, *mademoiselle*.'

Bonet seemed to hesitate. 'That is all science can ever do, *n'est-ce-pas*?'

'I want to see him.' Val stepped forward and brushed past Danielle impatiently. 'Where is he?'

'He is still in Recovery. He should be in his room in an hour or so. If you wish to wait. . .'

'Yes,' Danielle said quickly. 'Of course we'll wait.'

'Well, *I* can't wait, Danni.' Val pushed back her sleeve and glanced at her watch. 'They're shooting an important scene today. Barney's notified everybody to be on the set promptly at eight.'

Danielle stared at her cousin. 'Don't you want to be here when Lee awakens?'

Valerie shrugged her shoulders. 'Well, sure I do,' she said, giving Bonet a quick smile. 'But the doctor just said he's fine—isn't that right, Doctor? Didn't you say Lee's going to make it?'

The surgeon shifted his weight from one foot to the other. '*Oui*.'

'And his face won't be scarred or anything. Right?' Bonet nodded, and Valerie threw out her arms. 'So, what more is there to say? Lee's going to be OK.' She smiled. 'And that's great news. Barney will want to hear a first-hand report from me.'

'Lee might want to see a familiar face when he comes to,' Danielle said softly.

'Lee's a pro. He knows that the show has to go on.' Val glanced at her watch again. 'I can just about make it, if I leave now. What are you going to do, Danni? Do you want a lift or. . .?'

Danielle shook her head. 'You go ahead. I'll hang around for a while.'

Val's smile was gently pitying. 'Sure. You do that. I'll come by later, after they wrap up the shoot.'

Danielle waited until the staccato tap of her cousin's

heels had faded down the corridor, and then she turned to Dr Bonet.

'Could you ask someone to let me know when they bring Lee down from Recovery?' She smiled slightly. 'I'd just like to know he's. . .'

The doctor took her elbow. 'Permit me to take you to his room, Mademoiselle Nichols. Your wait will be more comfortable. And I am sure your friend will be glad to see a familiar face.'

Danielle shook her head. 'No,' she said quickly, 'I—I don't think he'll want to see me, Doctor. I——'

'Surely he will want to see the young woman who clung to him so—tenaciously—is that the right word?—all the way to the hospital.' Bonet smiled kindly. '*Mademoiselle*. Awakening after trauma is always difficult. Awakening in a strange place, seeing no face you know, hearing a tongue other than one's own—all that must be quite hard to bear, *n'est-ce-pas*?'

She nodded her head with reluctance. 'Yes, I suppose.'

'*Bien*. Come. I shall show you to your friend's room.'

The doctor's tone suggested there was nothing more to discuss. With a sigh of resignation, Danielle permitted him to lead her down the corridor.

'. . .over to the side. Get over, damn you! I'm losing it. Dammit, I can't. . .'

The rising sound of the husky, fear-roughened voice brought Danielle awake all at once. The room was striped with shadow, and a single light illuminated Lee's bed.

The magazine she'd tried to read hours earlier fell from her lap as she got to her feet and moved towards him. He was quiet now, asleep, but she knew he was still dreaming. She could see the movement of his eyes beneath his closed lids. There was a thin beading of sweat on his forehead.

She glanced at the clock on the wall near the door. How could she have slept so long? Hours had gone by since Lee had been wheeled into the room, his face ashen, tubes snaking into his arm, one leg wrapped in plaster and the other locked in what looked like a medieval torture device.

'He is still asleep,' one of the nurses had whispered in French. 'It may be quite some time before he awakens fully.'

Danielle had nodded, then settled in to wait. Someone had been kind enough to bring her coffee and something to read, but she'd had eyes only for Lee. He'd groaned softly a few times, and once his eyes had snapped open, only to close sightlessly again. The morning had dragged by, and the afternoon, and she'd found herself growing drowsy, nodding off, until finally. . .

'Danielle?'

Her heart turned over. Lee's eyes were open and fixed on her face.

'Lee.' She drew a deep breath, then let it out in a rush. 'How do you feel?'

'As if I've been run over by a truck,' he said. His mouth twisted, and she realised he was trying to smile. The smile became a grimace, and his breath hissed between his teeth. 'Bad joke,' he whispered.

'Are you in pain? I'll get the nurse. The doctor left orders——'

'No. No nurse. Not yet.' He grimaced again. 'I feel as if my mouth's stuffed with cotton.'

'Yes. They told me you'd be thirsty. Here—you can have a little water. Let me help you.'

Gently, Danielle put her arm around his shoulders and supported him as he drank. After a few seconds, he took his mouth from the straw and fell back against the pillows.

'Thanks.'

She nodded. 'Val—Val was here most of the night. She said to tell you——'

'I've been trying to count pieces,' he said. He cleared his throat and turned his face towards her. The smile that was not a smile drifted across his mouth again. 'All my parts seem to be here. Right?'

'Yes. You broke your ankle, and you banged up your knee. . .'

His eyes closed wearily. Danielle stood watching him, and then she carefully pushed back her chair and began tiptoeing from the room.

'Where are you going?'

His voice was soft, but it still rang with the old authority. She smiled slightly and turned back towards him.

'To tell the nurse you're awake. She'll want to——'

'The guy in the tractor. Is he OK?'

She nodded. 'Yes. He got away without a scratch.'

'Yeah, that's how it always goes. Somebody walks away, and somebody pays the price.' He drew in his breath. 'Jesus, I really did it this time, didn't I?'

'It wasn't your fault. That tractor. . .'

He looked at her, his eyes dark and unreadable. 'I screwed up,' he said flatly. 'In every possible way.' He hesitated. 'What about you?'

'Me?'

'Yes, you.'

She stared at him. 'I wasn't——'

'You must have seen what happened.'

Danielle touched her tongue to her lips. 'It was—it was upsetting.'

'Upsetting.' His voice was toneless, hoarse with exhaustion.

'I mean—I mean. . .' What she meant was that she'd almost died herself when she'd seen him lying there. But how could she tell him that?

The bed creaked as he tried to shift his weight. 'Do me a favour,' he said through his teeth. 'Call the nurse. Tell her I can use whatever happy juice she's got.' His breath hissed. 'And for Chrissakes, hurry.'

The days passed slowly. Val breezed in and out, but Danielle arranged her work schedule so she could spend most of each day at the hospital. Lee didn't know that, of course. She simply told him there wasn't very much happening on the set.

'So you figured if Val didn't need you, I might.' His voice was flat.

'My French is a hundred times better than yours,' she said easily. 'You'd still be trying to tell the nurse that you despise custard if I weren't here.'

A ghost of a smile flickered across his face. After a moment, he looked away.

'Suit yourself,' he said. 'You're a big girl.'

When reporters and photographers showed up in the lounge one day, Lee was reluctant to see them. But Val was there, and she insisted it was necessary.

'They'll think something's wrong if you turn them away,' she said, and finally he agreed.

'Five minutes, not a minute more,' he said. 'Just long enough to keep the sharks from thinking they can scent blood in the water.'

His photo was in the papers the next day, along with a brief story about his accident and his intention to be back on the racing circuit within two months.

Val's photo was there, too. Somehow, she'd managed to ease herself before the cameras each time the shutter had clicked.

Lee's pain lessened, but not his irritability. He was tired of lying around, he said, tired of being poked at, tired of taking medication.

'I'll decide when I need shots to ease the pain,' he growled.

Val thought that was wonderfully masculine. 'He's so macho,' she said, purring as she touched up her lipstick before going into Lee's room for one of her visits.

'It is not always beneficial to be so, as you say, macho,' Dr Bonet said, frowning as stepped into the hall. 'Things happen in life that require—how do you put it?—a perspectual difference.'

'A different perspective?' Danielle asked.

Bonet nodded. '*Oui.* Your friend should be encouraged to see himself as a total human being, not a superman.'

A little chill of premonition ran along Danielle's skin. Her eyes lifted to Val's, and her cousin made a face and rolled her eyes to the ceiling.

'Foreigners shouldn't try to speak like the rest of us,' she whispered after the surgeon was out of earshot.

But Danielle was barely listening. 'I'm going to talk to Bonet,' she began, and just then a covey of nurses swooped down on the two women. They wanted Lee's autograph on the magazine cover with his photo on it, they explained earnestly. Would Mademoiselle Nichols be so kind as to explain their request to Monsieur?

Danielle glanced down the hall, Bonet was waiting at the lift.

'*Mademoiselle*? Please, you will talk with him, yes?'

She looked from the nurses to the surgeon, just as the lift doors opened and Bonet stepped inside. Well, what did it matter? Bonet would be back tomorrow; she could speak to him then.

'*Oui,*' she said with a smile, and she led the little group into Lee's room.

But she missed seeing the doctor the next day and the day after that. His schedule had changed, she was told by the nurse in charge, he was making his rounds early in the mornings now. Was there, perhaps, a problem?

Danielle hesitated. There was no problem, not really, and finally she shook her head. After all, Bonet would have said something if there were. Lee was sitting up. Except for the paraphernalia on his legs, he even looked his old self again.

But his demeanour was changing, becoming almost grim. The exception was the day a group of men wearing satin jackets emblazoned with his name and his team's logo swarmed into his room and held court. He was all smiles that day—at least, until they left.

He said little for the remainder of the afternoon. His temper was short—Val showed up for one of her whirlwind visits and left even more quickly than usual.

'He's impossible,' she hissed as she hurried out of the door.

The next morning, Danielle paused at the nursing station. 'How is Mr Bradford today?' she asked.

The nurse raised her eyebrows. '*Formidable*.'

Danielle braced herself as she opened the door to Lee's room. Lee had graduated to sitting in a chair by the window for a brief time each morning and afternoon, and that was where he was now. 'Hi,' she said brightly. 'I got hold of a copy of last Sunday's *New York Times*. I thought you might——'

He turned towards her, his face glowering. 'I don't give a damn about the *Times*. I want to know when I'm going to get out of here.'

'And good morning to you, too,' she said with forced good cheer.

'I'm not in the mood for fun and games, Danielle. I'm damned tired of asking questions and getting no answers.'

Her smile faded. 'Have you asked questions?'

'Damned right I have. Bonet, the nurses. . .' He drew in his breath. 'All I do is ask questions. But everybody gets this blank look and starts examining the ceiling moulding or a floor tile.'

'Well, maybe they don't understand you.'

'Exactly. That's why I want you to go and find Bonet and talk to him.'

For some reason, Danielle felt as if the ground were tilting beneath her. 'Why don't you give it a day or two?' she said, turning away and busying herself with fluffing his pillows. 'You can't rush things, you know. I'm sure you'll be up and about soon. Until then——'

'Danielle. Look at me.' His voice was soft, and she knew she could no more deny him than she could walk on the moon. Her heart turned over when their eyes met. Under all that bluster, there was a darkness in his face that took her breath away. 'Please,' he said. 'Find Bonet. Talk to him. I just—I have this feeling that something's wrong.'

'Don't be silly. You broke your——'

'Dammit!' Lee slammed his hand on the arm of his chair. He glared at her, then took a deep breath. 'I know what I did,' he said in measured tones. 'Hell, I've broken bones before. But I've never had to lie around like a—a sack of potatoes while they knit.'

'All right,' she said softly. 'What do you want me to do?'

Lee lay his head back. He closed his eyes, then opened them again. 'Talk to Bonet. Ask him what the hell's going on. Tell him—tell him I'm going stir crazy, tell him I have to get out of here. . .'

His voice faded away. After a moment, Danielle nodded her head.

'I'll do the best I can.'

Her best was not good enough. Bonet avoided her questions. But he finally agreed to let Lee spend part of each day in a wheelchair.

'As for the rest, tell Monsieur Bradford I will be in to see him tomorrow.'

Danielle smiled when she brought Lee the news, smiled as she watched a burly attendant transfer him to the wheelchair. But the smile was false. All she could think of, as she wheeled him to the conservatory, was that Lee was right.

Something was terribly wrong.

CHAPTER SEVEN

VAL pushed open the door to Lee's room and smiled thinly. 'There you are, Danni. I spent the morning looking for you. I had stacks and stacks of mail that needed translating.' Her smile warmed as it fell on Lee. 'Hello, darling,' she purred. 'How are you feeling today?'

Lee's mouth turned down. 'Tired of issuing medical bulletins, that's how. Tell me how things are going on the set.'

Val sighed dramatically. 'All right, I suppose. Barney's being a bear—we're getting ready for the move to Monaco, and he's raging about everything.' She tucked her pale hair behind her ear as she sat down on the bed beside him. 'You'll be up and about by then, won't you, darling? On crutches or something?'

'I'd damned well better be. I've had enough of sitting on my tail to last a lifetime. I want out of here.'

'Who can blame you? And you will, indeed, leave us soon, Monsieur Bradford.' Dr Bonet's voice startled everyone. He smiled politely and inclined his head. 'Forgive me. I should have announced myself.'

'No,' Lee said quickly, 'come in, Doctor.' He hesitated. 'Did I hear you right? Did you say you're going to cut me loose?'

Bonet nodded. '*Oui*. I see no reason not to let you go within a few days. Being, as you say, up and about, however, may take some time.'

'I don't expect to run a marathon,' Lee said. He smiled, and Danielle thought it was the first real smile she'd seen on his face in days. 'All I want is to get up on some crutches or a cane or——'

'I am afraid that it not possible just yet, my friend.'

Lee puffed out his breath. 'Listen, Doc,' he said pleasantly, 'I know you guys get some kind of perverse kick out of keeping people bedridden. But this is only a broken leg, not some rare disease. You're just going to have to——'

'It is a fractured ankle, not a fractured leg.'

'Simpler still. Which is why there's no reason I can't——'

'This was a compound fracture, *monsieur*. There was nothing simple about it.' Bonet stepped into the room and closed the door. 'You have broken this ankle before, yes? Three, perhaps four years ago?'

'So?'

Bonet nodded thoughtfully. 'And then there is the knee injury, too. The ligament damage.'

'You told me all this already, Doc. I'm impressed, OK?'

'*Monsieur*, I think it is time we spoke of your injury in some depth.' He looked from one woman to the other, and raised his eyebrows enquiringly. 'Perhaps you would like the ladies to leave?'

Lee's laughter was strained. 'On the contrary. I think I'd better have them here as witnesses. Five minutes ago, you said I could check out of the hospital, but now you're waffling all over the place. Which is it, Doctor? Are you going to discharge me or aren't you?'

Bonet folded his arms and rocked back on his heels. 'I am going to discharge you, yes. If all continues to go well, you will be released within a few days.'

Lee's face lit with pleasure. 'All right!' he said, slapping his hand on his thigh. 'Val, tell Wexler I'll be on the set in Monaco within the week. And——'

Bonet shook his head. 'No, *monsieur*.'

'Ten days, then. And this cast has to come off within six weeks. I've a race in——'

The doctor cleared his throat. 'Monsieur Bradford, I think we do not understand each other. The cast is not a problem. It will come off, as you say, in six weeks, perhaps eight. You will need surgery in a year or so, to remove the plate and screws.'

'Come on, Doc. You don't expect me to sit on my hands for a year!'

'As to the knee,' the surgeon said, as if Lee hadn't spoken, 'the ligament was torn. I have sutured it. But——'

'Dr Bonet.' Lee's voice was quiet but it cut through the surgeon's words like a whip. 'Get to the bottom line. When do I get back on my feet?'

Danielle looked at the surgeon. Was it her imagination, or was Bonet hesitating, choosing his words very carefully before answering?

'You can begin to move around, on crutches,' he said finally, 'when the knee shows signs of healing.'

Lee grasped the bar in front of him with both hands. The muscles in his upper arms bunched beneath his tanned skin as he hoisted himself up in the bed. 'And when can I get back to my life, Doctor?' His voice was ominously soft. 'Because that's what we're really talking about, aren't we?'

Silence fell across the room. Danielle stared at the doctor. It wasn't her imagination, she thought suddenly. There was a grimness to the man's mouth that sent a warning chill racing along her spine. Something terrible was coming. Instinctively, she moved closer to Lee.

At first, Bonet's answer made no sense. 'There were reporters here last week, Monsieur Bradford. There was talk of you and a film, and I thought you must be an actor.'

Lee laughed, but the sound was forced. 'Not very likely, Doc. So if you're afraid to tell me that this scar over my eye is——'

'I know now that you are not an actor but a race-car driver. That is correct, no?'

'Yes. I race Formula One cars.'

The doctor nodded. '*Oui*,' he said, smiling a little. 'I have watched the sport often, *monsieur*, at Monaco. It surprises me that I did not associate your name with your profession.' He gave a Gallic shrug. 'I suppose it is that I think of my patients by ailment and not by name. You were the medial ligament of the left knee and the right ankle fracture. It is an unfortunate habit, but——'

'Doctor.' Lee drew in his breath, then let it out slowly. 'Please,' he said. 'Cut the crap and get to it.'

Bonet cleared his throat again. 'Let us start with the ankle. It has already been weakened, yes? The bones of the leg—the fibula and tibia, and the malleolus processes—are just above the astragalus——'

'Damn it, man!' Lee leaned forward, his eyes locked on the surgeon's face. 'Just say it.'

Bonet seemed to draw himself together. 'I am afraid you shattered the bones at the ankle joint, my friend. We were left with nothing but fragments.'

Val's chair clattered against the wall as she shoved it back and rose to her feet.

'I'll be outside,' she said, but no one looked at her. Danielle moved closer to Lee and put her hand on his shoulder. The tension in him drove into her flesh like an electric current.

'Fragments,' the doctor said, 'which, try as we might, could not be put back together as God had made them. If it had only been your hip, *monsieur*—we have a very fine hip replacement today, as good or perhaps better than the orig——'

Lee's breath hissed in his throat. 'Are you telling me I'm not going to walk again?'

'No,' the doctor said quickly. 'No, my friend, you will

walk.' He paused, and his eyes sought Lee's. 'You will limp,' he said, very deliberately. 'But you will walk.'

Lee's mouth twisted, and then he gave a tight smile. 'I can live with that.'

'But your ankle will be locked in one position.' Bonet's voice was cold and professional, although Danielle thought she had never seen greater compassion in a man's face before. 'It will not rotate, it will not flex. As for the knee—the ligament will heal. But the knee will not be strong. It will not be able to take any abuse at all. Walking, yes. But prolonged stress. . .' He spread his arms in a gesture of supplication. 'Do you understand?'

Danielle felt Lee's body grow rigid beneath her hand. She looked at him and then at the surgeon. Bonet had promised an explanation of Lee's injuries, but this had gone too far. One look at Lee's tortured face was enough to tell her that.

She wanted to speak up, to say that *she* didn't understand. But she was an intruder here. Bonet's words had somehow destroyed Lee, and it seemed almost obscene that she should witness it.

The sound of Lee's indrawn breath rasped in the sudden silence. 'I don't believe you,' he said flatly. 'There are other doctors, other treatments.'

'I wish that were true, my friend. But there are not. Even if I had known your profession, I could have done nothing more.'

Lee twisted free of Danielle's hand. 'When can I get out of here?' he said harshly. His face, under its tan, was as white as the bed linen.

'As I said, there is no sense in keeping you hospitalised, Monsieur Bradford. You will probably mend more quickly away from our sterile surroundings. Perhaps there is a quiet place to which you can go and someone to help you?'

'A nurse to wipe my bottom? Is that what you mean?'

Bonet's eyebrows rose. 'I know this is not the news you would have wished for, *monsieur*. But there are those who do not survive crashes such as the one you had. You should be grateful that——'

'Spare me the speeches, Doctor.'

'Monsieur Bradford, I understand how you feel. But——'

Lee's eyes blazed with cold fury. 'Don't patronise me, Bonet. You have no idea how I feel.'

'But I do. I have given you a bleak prognosis, and——'

'Just get out of here,' Lee said, pulling away from Danielle's hand. 'Go on, get out.'

There was no mistaking his anger. But Danielle could hear something else in his voice, pain or perhaps something more. She leaned towards him, her eyes searching his face.

'Lee,' she said, 'please. . .'

'Didn't you hear me? I said to get out.'

The doctor's hand pressed lightly on Danielle's shoulder. After a moment, she turned reluctantly and followed him into the hall.

Val stepped forward as the door to Lee's room swung shut. Her eyes were shiny with excitement. 'I heard it all,' she whispered, looking from Danielle to the doctor. 'But I don't understand. Why is he so upset?'

Bonet sighed as they walked down the corridor to the lift. 'Racing is a very demanding sport. Perhaps you do not think of the driver as an athlete, but that is what he is.' He hesitated. 'And the legs—the legs must be strong. The right foot moves from accelerator to brake, the left operates the clutch. Smoothly, yes? And quickly.'

'Well, so what?' Danielle said tersely. 'Lee's legs are fixed. You did all those things to them. What's the——'

Danielle stumbled to a halt as the implication of Bonet's words became clear. But she didn't want to believe it. Her eyes pleaded with him to tell her she was wrong. Instead, he nodded his head.

'*Oui*, Mademoiselle Nichols, I am afraid that is correct. Your friend's ankle and knee may no longer stand up under such stress.'

Val frowned as she looked at the doctor. 'I'm not into mind-reading,' she said impatiently. 'Would somebody please tell me what's going on here?'

Danielle drew a ragged breath. 'Lee. . .' Her voice broke. 'Lee's not going to race any more. That's right, isn't it, Doctor?'

Bonet sighed. 'I am not God. But I am afraid that may be so.'

'That's crazy.' Valerie snorted. 'It's crazy, I tell you. All he's done is break an ankle and tear a something-or-other. People do worse all the time.'

The doctor shook his head. 'I am sorry, *mademoiselle*.'

Valerie stared at him. 'You don't understand,' she whispered after a moment. 'He's on the top. He's the best.'

Danielle put her hand on the other woman's arm. 'Never mind that now. We have to see to it he gets well. He needs—he needs. . .'

Val drew herself together. 'Yes. A month in the country and somebody to hold his hand. I told you, I heard it all.' She turned towards the lift and stabbed the call button with her finger. 'All right,' she said briskly, 'I'll see to it. I'll contact his manager and tell him he has to rent a cottage and hire a nurse.'

Danielle stared at her. Surely Val had misunderstood.

'He needs someone to help him, Val. Someone who cares. You said that you cared, you said——'

'And he'll have someone. Dr Bonet will help us hire a good nurse, won't you, Doctor?'

'Dammit, Val.' Danielle's voice rose. 'He needs more than that. You can't turn your back on him now.'

'Just don't get so wound up, Danni. *I* can't baby-sit him. I can't even stand the sight of blood—you know that.' Val clenched her jaw. 'Where is that damned lift?' she muttered, stabbing at the button again. 'And I have my job to consider. Barney—Mr Wexler—said he might consider me for a walk-on part. It's not much, but. . .' The door to the lift hissed open and she stepped quickly inside. 'We're leaving for Monaco in two days, Danni. You'd better come back to Ste Agathe tonight and get your things packed.'

Danielle slumped back against the wall as the lift door closed. 'She won't help him,' she said in disbelief. 'My God, I knew she was self-centred, but. . .'

The doctor smiled reassuringly. 'Please, do not worry, *mademoiselle*. I have a friend who operates a very pleasant sanatorium in the mountains. Monsieur Bradford will have a private room and all the therapy his legs demand.'

'Lee? In a sanatorium?' She laughed sharply. 'How are you going to get him there, Doctor? By tying him down and stuffing him into a cage?'

Dr Bonet shuffled his feet. 'He is angry and upset now. But in a day or so, when he is in a more reasonable frame of mind. . .'

She drew in her breath, then let it out slowly. 'He doesn't need nursing care, does he? Professional care, I mean.'

'He will need someone to see to it he exercises and eats properly, someone to try and improve his frame of mind. . .' The surgeon's eyes swept her face. 'Ah, *mademoiselle*,' he said softly, 'I see what is in your heart. But it would not be wise. Your friend will be a very difficult patient.'

'You just said he wouldn't need professional care.' Danielle lifted her chin resolutely. 'I'm more than capable of changing a dressing or running a tub.'

'Mademoiselle Nichols, why would you undertake such a responsibility?'

Why? Yes—that was a good question. But she didn't want to try and answer it. Not yet.

Her eyes met Bonet's. 'It just—it just seems the right thing to do.'

'My dear young woman, Monsieur Bradford's greatest problem will not be a medical one, it will be a psychological one. He must come to terms with himself, and I suspect the cost of that will be high. Do you understand?'

'I know it isn't going to be easy for him. But——'

'It would not be easy for you, either. It would take great strength on your part, Mademoiselle Nichols. I cannot emphasise how difficult a task this would be. Promise me you will think twice before committing yourself to such a scheme.'

She did think about it—and the more she thought, the more she knew she wanted to do it. All she had to do was convince Lee to agree with her.

She wasn't foolish enough to talk of nursing him back to health. Instead, she told him she had a proposition to make, one that would benefit the both of them. She wanted to go home, she said, her summer wasn't working out very well.

'Val and I haven't been getting along. We don't have much in common.'

That, at least, was the truth. Lee looked at her, and for an instant the anger left his eyes.

'No,' he said softly, 'I suppose you don't.' His face closed again, shadowed and cold. 'What about your obligation to Wexler?'

'Mr Wexler's found a translator to replace the one who quit. He can do his job and mine with one hand tied behind his back, now that they're leaving Ste Agathe for Monaco.'

'Well, what's any of this got to do with me?'

Now came the hard part. 'I thought we might help each other out,' she said briskly. 'I need a job.'

'I thought you said you wanted to go home.'

'That's right. I do. But my plane ticket's one of those discount things. It's not good until the end of summer. So I thought—I thought you and I. . .' Her courage almost failed her at the sudden glowering look in Lee's eyes. 'I thought we'd help each other out. You need someone to give you a hand the next few weeks and I need a job. Do you see what I'm getting at?'

'No,' he said bluntly, although she was sure he was lying. He knew, all right, he was just trying to force her to spell it out.

'What I'm suggesting is that we combine forces. I don't need a salary, just room and board. And you. . .'

'. . .need a nurse. Did you and the sawbones work this out together?'

'I'd be there to help out if you needed me,' Danielle said, ignoring the challenge in his words. 'I could drive you around, do your shopping—that kind of thing.'

'Forget it. I'll give you the money for another ticket.'

'I'm not looking for a hand-out, Lee. If I want charity, I can get it elsewhere.'

His teeth flashed in a cold parody of a smile. 'I see,' he said softly, 'so you're not a beggar.'

'No, I'm not. That's why I'm suggesting this arrangement. Maybe we can help each other.'

'Maybe you have a thing for cripples.'

His words made her wince, but she kept her composure. 'I'm not even going to dignify that with a response,' she said.

'Maybe you just get off on being used.'

She knew he was hurting, that it was the reason for his cruelty. But something in his caustic remark touched a raw nerve.

'Maybe you just like being a bastard,' she said before she could stop herself. Her hand flew to her mouth. 'God, I'm sorry. I didn't mean. . .'

For a second, a spark of light glowed in Lee's eyes. 'Don't apologise,' he said. 'I deserved that.' The glint faded as quickly as it had appeared, and he turned his face to the wall. 'All right,' he said. There was a terrible weariness in his voice. 'Have it your way. What the hell—Bonet won't cut me loose until he's satisfied I'm going to get what he refers to as "proper care", and that seems to come down to a sanatorium staffed by the Little Sisters of Mercy or you. Given that, what choice do I have?'

Danielle felt her heart slam against her ribs. 'I'll take care of everything,' she said, trying to sound calm. 'I'll find someplace quiet—it's lovely in the mountains near Grasse, they say, and. . .'

Lee turned towards her again, his eyes as emotionless as a shark's. 'Spare me the details. Just make it someplace the newshounds can't find. I'm not about to let anybody see me like this.' He clamped his teeth together, then reached to the bedside table, yanked open the top drawer, and pulled out a cheque-book and pen. 'Here,' he said, scribbling his name furiously, 'spend whatever you need. Arrange for a car, a house, a staff—whatever it takes to get me out of this place.'

Danielle's hand brushed his as she took the cheques. His skin was cool and dry, as if he had aged in the past weeks.

'You won't regret this, Lee, I promise.'

The coldness of his stare silenced her. 'Don't make promises you can't keep,' he said, and then he turned his back to her.

Valerie was incredulous when Danielle told her what she was going to do. 'What kind of nonsense is this,

Danni? I told you, we'll get Lee a place to stay and a nurse, and——'

'It's all settled, Val. I'm not changing my mind.'

Her cousin gaped at her, bewildered. 'You can't do this to me.'

'I'm not "doing" anything to you. Lee needs someone to look after him.'

'And what about me?' Val's voice rose stridently. 'Barney doesn't like his new translator very much. He keeps asking when you'll be back. And—and he keeps reminding me that I fudged my credentials when he hired me.'

Danielle smiled sympathetically. 'I wish I could help you.'

'You can. Just come to your senses.' Val smiled. 'After all, you're my cousin. My favourite. . .'

The old litany fell on Danielle's ears like a chord played on an out of tune piano. 'It won't work this time,' she said quietly. 'I'm sorry, Val.'

The look of wide-eyed innocence slipped from Valerie's face. 'You're as transparent as glass,' she said coldly. 'You've got a schoolgirl crush on Lee, that's what this is all about.'

'That isn't true,' Danielle said quickly.

The pretty face grew hard as stone. 'Lee always did know how to make the most of his groupies—although I suppose that's the wrong word to use now. You won't have much competition, now that he's a cripple.'

Danielle caught her breath. 'How can you call him that?'

'You'd never have a chance if he were still a whole man. You and I both know that.'

Danielle stared at her cousin. She'd had glimpses of the woman behind the pretty mask before, but she had never seen her as clearly as she did at this moment.

'Think what you like, Val,' she said softly. 'I really don't give a damn.'

Val's mouth dropped open. She looks like a fish, Danielle thought unkindly. I've really shocked her.

The realisation brought a surprisingly fierce rush of pleasure.

The next days were a blur. The nurses taught her to change the dressing on Lee's knee and to organise his medications. Dr Bonet recommended an estate agent who listened to Danielle in silence, then beamed and pulled a photograph from a stack on his desk.

'*La parfaite maisonnette*,' he said happily.

It was hard to tell anything from the snapshot. The 'perfect cottage' was a dark smudge set within a darker blur.

'*Regardez*,' the agent said. '*Des oliviers*.'

Olive trees. Well, that would be nice. Actually, all that mattered was that the cottage met the requirements she'd drawn up: there was, the agent assured her, a bedroom and toilet for Lee on the ground floor as well as similar accommodations for her on the upper level, there were wide french doors that would accommodate Lee's wheelchair, and it was far enough from any city to ensure his privacy.

She sighed the lease agreeent on the spot and hurried back to the hospital with the blurred photo in her pocket.

Lee refused even to look at it, just as he had refused to be drawn into any of the planning.

'Do as you like,' he said each time she sought his opinion. 'I don't care, one way or the other.'

But Danielle sensed that wasn't entirely true. She had the feeling he was weighing each action she took, waiting for her plans to collapse in ruins.

He was silent as a male orderly helped him into the car the day he was discharged from the hospital, and he remained silent as Danielle pulled away from the kerb. His back was rigid as he sat beside her, his legs—one in a cast, the other fitted out with a metal brace—stretched beneath the dashboard.

'Well,' she said brightly, 'here we go. I hope there won't be much traffic on the autoroute.'

Lee didn't answer.

'I have a map there, on the dash. The estate agent marked the route for us—I thought you might——'

'I'm sure you're capable of finding the way.'

It was the last thing he said for the next hour and a half. By then, her hands were sweating with tension.

She hadn't really expected to feel as if they were setting out on a holiday. But she'd let herself hope Lee might loosen up a little as they left the hospital and then the city behind them. The rolling countryside was beautiful, dotted with small farms and vineyards. The air was clean and fresh, and the sun was sweet on the land.

But Lee didn't react to any of it. He sat staring out of the windscreen in unblinking silence, never once looking at her or acknowledging her presence.

They left the autoroute finally and followed a twisting secondary road until she found the turn-off the agent had marked on the map. Now they were on a route so narrow it was little more than a track. Danielle slowed the car, but it bounced heavily on the rutted surface. She winced as, from the corner of her eye, she glimpsed Lee's legs jounce against the dashboard.

'Sorry,' she said, gripping the wheel more tightly.

The road smoothed for a bit, then grew rutted again. The car dipped into a shallow depression, then jogged up the other side. Lee gave a soft grunt of pain.

'Sorry,' Danielle said again. 'I'm trying not to——'

'It's all right.'

'Is your leg bothering you? I can stop for a while, if——'

'I said it was all right.'

'If it hurts, why don't you take a pill for the pain? There's a flask of water in the glove compartment, and——'

Lee glared at her. 'Maybe Valerie likes having you play Mother Hen. But I find it distasteful.'

She swallowed. 'I was just trying to——'

'I'll make a deal with you,' he said coldly. 'Don't give me medical advice and I won't tell you how to drive this damned car. How does that sound?'

Danielle nodded. 'I'm sorry. I only meant——'

He slammed his fist against the dashboard. 'And for God's sake, stop apologising. Just get us to this God-forsaken nursing home you've rented. Where the hell is it, anyway? If we go much further, we'll be in Italy.'

Her hands gripped the steering-wheel tightly. Lee was spoiling for a quarrel, but she wasn't going to oblige. What chance would she have of helping him if things started off badly?

'We should be there soon,' she said. The calmness in her voice pleased her. 'The agent said to look for a cottage, on a hilltop. He said it was very old, four or five hundred years actually, and that there's a red tile roof and——'

Lee shifted in his seat. 'Is that it?'

Danielle followed his pointing finger. At first, she saw nothing but olive trees. Then, through a break in their heavily leafed branches, she glimpsed stone walls and red tile.

'Maybe.' She crossed her fingers mentally as she turned on to the road that led into olive grove. 'Let's take a closer look.'

They had arrived. She knew it even before they pulled up before the house. The agent had described everything perfectly: the trees, the old house itself, the overgrown garden off to the side, even the stately row of cypresses that stood beyond to shelter the cottage from the hot wind that began life across the distant Mediterranean.

Danielle shut off the engine and silence settled around the car. There was a feeling of great tranquillity here. In some way she couldn't fathom, she felt as if she had come home.

Lee's voice shattered the peaceful moment. 'Well? Is this our little paradise or isn't it?'

She drew a deep breath, then gave him a false smile. 'It is, if the key fits,' she said, fumbling at her seatbelt.

It did, as she was certain it would. The door swung open to a cool, shadowy interior relieved by whitewashed walls and beamed ceilings. She stood still for a moment, and then a smile curved across her lips and she hurried back to the car.

'It's lovely,' she said, lifting Lee's wheelchair from the boot. 'There's a huge fireplace, and a slate staircase, and——'

Lee grasped his right leg and swung it out of the car door. 'And steps leading in. Or didn't you notice?'

'Yes, but only two. Inside——'

'There'd better be a bedroom and a lavatory on the first floor.'

'Here,' she said, reaching towards him. 'Let me help you.'

He brushed her hand away. 'Don't touch me,' he said, his voice sharp. 'I can manage by myself. All you have to do is get that damned chair close to the car and hold it steady.' He grunted as he lifted his other leg free, then hoisted himself into the chair. 'Now call someone to get me up the steps.'

Danielle ran her tongue across her lips. 'I can do it,' she said. 'The nurses showed me how.'

Lee glared at her, his eyes dark with impatience. 'Get someone, I said. The housekeeper or——'

'There—there isn't anyone. There's just me.'

He looked at her as if she'd gone mad. 'What the hell are you talking about? I told you to hire a staff. A housekeeper. A cook. A man to move me. Why didn't you?'

Danielle swallowed hard. Where was all her resolve to be strong? she thought unhappily. But she knew where it was; it lay somewhere behind them, stripped away by the long drive and by Lee's cold silence.

She forced herself to breathe deeply, then met his eyes. 'The estate agent arranged for a woman to clean and do laundry. As for the rest—you were concerned about your privacy, the newspapers and all that. I—I thought it would be best if we—you said you wanted to be alone, and you will be. Except for me, of course. . .'

Her words drifted away. There was more to it, she thought suddenly, and she'd never acknowledged it until this moment.

Lee had insisted on privacy. But he'd never talked about being alone. It was she who'd wanted that, she who wanted to recapture the intimacy they'd shared for that fraction of time the day they'd met and again during those dizzying moments just before—just before. . .

The chair squealed in protest as Lee grasped the wheels and began propelling himself towards the door.

'This will be the first and last time you drag me up those bloody steps. First thing tomorrow, drive into town and hire someone to help out. Do you hear me?'

Danielle nodded as she followed slowly after him. 'Yes,' she said softly, 'I hear you.'

But what she was really listening to, with an intensity that alarmed her, was the sudden loud clamour of her own heart.

CHAPTER EIGHT

But there was no chance to go to town the next day or the day after. Rain fell in endless sheets from a pewter sky, turning the rutted dirt roads to oozing mud. Driving would have been difficult, if not impossible.

By the time the clouds moved off and the sun shone again, it was obvious, even to Lee, that they really didn't need anyone else. The cleaning woman was the wife of a local farmer; she arranged for delivery of cheese and eggs, meat and produce, all brought to the door by donkey cart. Danielle cooked simple meals, which she and Lee ate in silence at a scarred wooden table before the fireplace or on the terrace, viewing an overgrown garden that scented the air with rosemary, sage, and lavender.

And all around stood the olive trees, silvery sentinels through which the wind blew its hot breath.

The cottage and its grounds were, as the agent had promised, lovely. But, as the days passed, Danielle's initial delight in the place diminished. The charm of the exposed-beam ceilings and whitewashed stone walls wasn't strong enough to stand up to the tension that settled over the house.

Lee spoke only when necessary, and then in monosyllabic grunts that discouraged any further conversation. After a while, Danielle began spinning a mindless chatter about the house and its grounds, but he paid no attention. Sometimes he wheeled his chair out of the room while she was in the middle of a sentence; sometimes he just sat unhearing and stared off into space.

Watching him from the corner of her eye while he sat

that way, Danielle thought about the active life he'd led. How much longer could he go on like this? It was as if the essence of him were fading away. Sooner or later, there'd be nothing left of Lee Bradford but a shadow.

She told herself there had to be some way to occupy him. But nothing worked—he paid no attention to the old radio that picked up static-filled broadcasts from Italy and Switzerland, or to the old phonograph and stack of scratchy records that dated back to the sixties.

Danielle wished she'd thought to bring along some books or even a deck of playing-cards. She searched the cupboards and shelves without success. Finally, one morning, she pulled down the overhead ladder that led to the attic and climbed the rungs to a dark, airless space crammed with boxes and old furniture.

An hour later, sneezing from the dust, she emerged triumphantly clutching a chess set and half a dozen yellowing books.

She dusted everything off, then marched into the living-room carrying the chess set. Lee was sitting near the window, looking out at the dark green cypress trees.

'Look what I found.' Her voice was determinedly cheerful. She waited, and finally he turned and looked at her. She held up the board, and his dull glance fell on it. 'Do you play?' she asked. He gave an imperceptible nod, as if it took all his energy to do so. 'Well,' she said brightly, 'so do I. Why don't we. . .?'

He turned away before she'd finished the suggestion. She tried the books next, presenting them for Lee's approval with a flourish and an artificial smile.

'What shall we try? Colette? Voltaire? De Maupassant? They're in French, of course, but I can——'

'I'm sure you can,' he said coldly. 'But I'm not interested.'

'Lee.' Danielle's smile fled and she took a step towards him. 'You can't just——'

'Leave me alone.'

'Lee, please—listen to me. This isn't healthy. You. . .'

She stumbled back as he rolled past her, the wheels of his chair barely missing her toes. The exchange between them marked some kind of progress, she thought unhappily. It was the most he had spoken in days.

His message was absolutely clear. Leave me alone, he was saying, I don't want any part of you.

Dr Bonet had said it would take great strength to help him, and Danielle had glibly assured him she had that strength. Now she was no longer certain.

Lee's body was healing. She could see the improvement in his knee each time she dressed it, just as she knew that the bones in his ankle were knitting beneath his cast. But his spirit was not. If anything, it seemed to be deteriorating.

It wasn't hard to figure out what was happening. Lee's world had come apart. The unknown lay ahead, and it terrified him. It was how she'd felt years ago, when her parents had died. One day, your life was moving ahead and the next, it lay shattered around you, and when you looked at the pieces you no longer cared what tomorrow might bring.

Her heart went out to him. Filled with compassion, sometimes her throat tightened just watching him stare into the untended garden during the long afternoons, or into the blazing fire during the even longer evenings.

But compassion, to Danielle's surprise, was not an emotion that gave her much comfort. She began to feel edgy, almost irritable. It was all this inactivity, she told herself. She wasn't used to it.

She began poking through the cottage and its grounds, searching for something to occupy the dragging hours. There was an old shed behind the house; it was thick with dust and cobwebs, but tucked away in a corner she found a basket of garden tools.

She squatted down and lifted out a rusty trowel. A smile flickered across her face. She hadn't gardened in years, but she'd always liked it. Well, not always. A city child until she'd gone to live with Aunt Helen and Uncle John, she'd thought that vegetables started life in the supermarket.

The Cummingses lived in the country. And they had a garden in which rows of carrots, cabbages, and lettuces marched neatly side by side. The first time Aunt Helen had sent her to pull some carrots for dinner, she'd been wide-eyed with amazement.

'You mean, all this grows behind your house?' she'd said to Val.

Val had shot her a scornful look. 'Yes, silly. What did you think?'

'I don't know what I thought. I just never—gee, it's wonderful, isn't it? Planting your own carrots, watching them grow. . .'

'. . .picking off the bugs, getting your hands all dirty.' Val had shuddered. 'If you think it's so great, you can help my father keep his dumb garden instead of me from now on.'

It had been the first of Val's chores she'd taken over, and the only one she'd truly wanted. Uncle John was an uncommunicative man, and he never said much even while they worked side by side in the garden. But Danielle had loved feeling useful; she'd loved, even more, the pleasures of working the soil. It was lovely to feel the heat of the sun on your shoulders and honest sweat on your skin. And there was a very special pleasure in seeing something come to life and thrive under your touch.

It would, she thought now, be nice to feel that way

again. Carefully, she brushed the dust and spider-webs from the old tools.

She started working in the overgrown garden that afternoon. Sweat dripped from her face and her muscles ached from the unaccustomed exertion, but it felt wonderful to be doing something useful. It made Lee's continuing moodiness easier to bear—at first. But, as the days passed, not even hours of weeding and hoeing relieved the tension Danielle felt building within her.

Something foreign to her nature was eclipsing her compassion. It was days before she could force herself to name it.

Anger. What she felt for Lee was anger.

In the quiet of her bedroom, she stared at herself in the mirror. 'You must be crazy,' she whispered to her reflection. 'Only a crazy woman could be angry at a man in a wheelchair.'

But no matter what she told herself, the feeling grew. She felt ugly words bottled up within her that might, without warning, spill from her lips.

She decided it might be best to take a page from Lee's book and say nothing at all. She gave up her mindless attempts at conversation, becoming, instead, as silent as he.

Her days were given over to the garden. Sage and lavender had survived long neglect, and she even unearthed phlox struggling for survival under a scraggly cover of weed. Her nights were spent with her nose buried in the books she'd once offered to read aloud. Not that she was really reading—the French words might as well have been Sanskrit as they danced across the page without meaning.

Then, one evening, a log snapped in the fireplace. Danielle looked up—and found Lee watching her. It was the first time they'd made eye contact in a long time, and it was disconcerting. The expression on his face rattled her, too. He was looking at her in a way that told her he'd been doing it for some time.

She blinked and looked back to her book. But she could feel his gaze burning her skin. Say something to him, she thought. 'Did you—did you want something?'

He shook his head. 'No.'

Then why was he still staring at her?

'Are you sure? I—I could make some tea, if you like, or coffee.' He didn't answer, he just kept looking at her. 'There are cookies, too, left over from——'

Lee's eyes narrowed. 'Well,' he said softly, 'it's not deathless conversation, but it's better than nothing.'

Colour rose to her cheeks. 'What's that supposed to mean?'

'I tried telling you this wouldn't work. But you wouldn't listen.'

'I don't know what——'

'Don't give me that. You've been moping around here for days.'

She stared at him. 'I haven't been moping.'

'Yes, you have. And why not? This place is a—a damned morgue.'

Danielle closed her book. 'I'm sorry you feel that way. It seems like a very nice——'

'What the hell else can it be, when you're locked away here, taking care of a cripple?'

A little knot of tension began forming in her belly. 'I haven't complained,' she said calmly. 'And you're not a cripple. You'll be up and about soon.'

'With a beggar's cup in my hand.'

'With a life to live. If you'd only——'

'Are you really that dense?' His eyes were as cold as midnight. 'I won't be racing any more. That's what Bonet——'

'You *might* not race any more. *That's* what he said.'

Lee gave his chair a hard shove backwards. 'What do you know about it, little girl?'

'I know that it's not enough to sit and brood. And——'

'Ah. The little farm girl offers advice. How charming.'

Danielle took a deep breath. 'I've asked you not to call me that.'

His face twisted. 'What's the matter, Danielle? Don't you like the way people talk in the real world?'

Her hand shook as she placed her book on the table. Then she rose from her chair and started towards the living-room door. Lee's voice roared after her.

'Where the bloody hell do you think you're going?'

He was trying to pick a fight. But she wasn't going to let him.

'To bed,' she said. 'It's been a long day.'

Lee snorted. 'Go on,' he said, 'run, little girl. Reality's too much for you. I knew it would be.'

Danielle took a deep breath. 'Look,' she said, 'there's not much sense in——'

'Go on,' he said, disgust coating each word, 'get out. Go dream your sweet dreams.'

'Damn you, Lee Bradford!' She spun towards him, her hazel eyes bright with rage. 'Don't you dare talk to me that way.'

An electric silence seemed to crackle in the shadowed room. She stared at him, and then she took a step forward.

'You're so wrapped up in yourself,' she said, fighting to stay calm, 'that you think you're the only one who's ever had your world turned upside-down.'

Lee turned his chair away, then waved his hand in contemptuous dismissal. 'Yeah, I've heard that life is tough all over.'

Danielle strode across the room and stepped in front of him. Her hands went to her hips. 'That's right,' she said, 'it is.'

His lip curled. 'What's this going to be, a speech about how lucky I am to be alive? Forget it. I've heard it all before.'

'No. No speech. Someone as selfish as you wouldn't listen.'

His arrogant smile faded. 'Selfish?' he said in a dangerous whisper. 'Is that what you think?'

'Do you really care what I think?'

Lee drew a rasping breath. 'I—I. . .' There was a long silence, and then he looked down. 'No,' he growled, 'why should I?'

'If you think you're the only one who's been alone and hurting. . .'

He laughed. 'Don't tell me. You didn't get voted Homecoming Queen. Or maybe you didn't have a date for the Senior Prom——'

Her voice sliced across his with frigid clarity. 'My father died when I was eleven. And before the year was out, my mother was dead, too. I was sent to live with Val and her parents.'

Slowly, she sank down on the edge of the sofa. Her eyes met Lee's. He was watching her as if he'd never seen her before.

'That,' she said softly, as much to herself as to him, 'was my introduction to what you call reality.'

Lee cleared his throat. 'I'm sorry. I didn't know. Val never——'

Danielle gave a shrug. 'Why would she? It wasn't anything momentous to her. She was busy with her own life—she's always been busy with her own life. I don't think she noticed me much at first, except when I got in her way.'

She fell silent again. The memories were flowing back, still painful after all these years. In some still-rational part of her mind, a bemused voice was demanding to know what she thought she was doing. But it was too late to stop—for one thing, the knot in her stomach was easing as she spoke.

'OK.' His voice was gruff. 'OK. It must have been rough. But——'

'Rough?' Danielle shook her head. 'I was eleven years old, Lee. I was just a child.' Her voice trembled. 'There's no way to describe how alone I felt.'

Lee's chair cltterd over the tile floor as he wheeled towards her. 'All right,' he said. 'I was wrong. You know what it is to hurt. But——'

Danielle's eyes lifted to his. 'That's not what this is about.' She took a deep breath, then reached out and embraced the truth. 'This—this is about giving up.'

'Quitting,' he said with distaste.

She nodded. 'Giving up, quitting—call it what you like.' She touched her tongue to her lips. 'I'm an expert at it. It's what I did, for a long time. My world was gone, and—and I had a choice between facing what came next head on or—or crawling inside myself and hiding.'

Lee put his hand on hers. 'You were just a kid,' he said softly.

'So I hid,' she said, dismissing his platitudes. 'I ignored my own life, I stood back while everybody else. . .' Her eyes flashed to his. 'It took me years to see it and to change.' There was steel in her voice. 'But you're not a child, Lee, you're an adult in the prime of his life. Don't let the time slip away from you.'

He snatched his hand from hers. 'Here we go,' he said coldly. 'It's a speech, after all.'

'No.' The smile she gave him was twisted. 'Just some advice—from one expert on giving up to another.'

He recoiled from her words as if she'd struck him. The breath hissed betwee his teeth. 'You don't know what you're saying,' he said angrily. 'I just want to be left alone. Is that so difficult to——?'

'Damn you, Lee Bradford!' Danielle's voice exploded into the room. 'Just listen to yourself. Quitting is quitting, no matter how you try and explain it.'

Her heart felt as if it were breaking when she saw the pain that flashed across his face. But there was no calling back what she'd said. She had come here to help him get well, but the next move was his. There were some kinds of healing that could only come from within.

They stared at each other in silence. Then Lee's face twisted in rage. He reached out and caught her wrist. His fingers compressed the fragile bones, but she forced herself not to flinch.

'I'm not a coward, damn you,' he said in a ragged whisper. 'I've never run from anything in my life.'

'I didn't call you a coward,' Danielle said softly.

'I know what you called me. And I don't like it.'

'Something terrible happened to you, Lee.' Her voice was low, her gaze steady. 'Now you have a choice. You can face up to it or you can curl up inside yourself, as I did. And if you do that—if you do. . .'

All at once, her composure slipped away. She began to weep—for the lost child she'd been, for the despairing man he was. Lee cursed softly, and then his arms closed around her.

'I—I don't know why I'm crying,' she sobbed. 'I—I. . .'

'It's all right,' he murmured. 'Let go. I'm here. I've got you.'

She held herself rigid for a moment more. But Lee's arms were warm and comforting. She felt safe, in a way she never had before. With a muffled cry, she slid from the sofa to her knees beside him. Lee whispered her name, then gathered her to him with a tenderness that took her breath away. Her arms went around his neck and she buried her face in his shoulder.

'Don't cry,' he crooned, stroking her hair. 'Please don't cry.'

Tears trickled from under her lashes. 'You have to fight back,' she whispered, leaning back in his arms and looking into his eyes. 'Do you understand? Otherwise—otherwise. . .'

'Hush.' Lee kissed her temple, then pressed his lips to the shining curls on the top of her head. He drew her against him again, and she closed her eyes. After a long while, he took a shuddering breath. 'All right,' he said softly, 'we'll make a deal.'

Danielle sniffed damply. 'No medical advice from me, no driving lessons from you.' She drew back and gave him a shaky smile. 'That was the deal we made the day we drove here, remember?'

He smiled. 'You did just fine with your end—but I suspect I could have used some advice from time to time.'

She smiled back at him. 'Is this bargain going to be different?'

'Yes.' He took a deep breath. 'I'll try if you'll help me.' His hands cupped her face. 'How does that sound?'

'It sounds—it sounds fine,' she murmured.

He nodded solemnly. 'Let's shake on it.'

Danielle put her hand in his. 'All right.'

'Danielle.' His whisper hung in the sudden silence, and then he gathered her to him and kissed her.

It was a tender kiss, one that brushed her lips with the taste of honey. His next kiss was harder, and suddenly he groaned and his mouth closed over hers in passionate demand.

Kneeling before him, lost in the magic of his embrace, Danielle responded, returning kiss for kiss with an abandon she had never before known.

His fingers closed on the top button of her shirt and slid it open, then moved to the next. Suddenly, his hand stilled. 'Danielle?' Her eyes opened slowly and focused on his face. 'I want to make love to you,' he said softly.

The whispered words drove a flood of heat to her cheeks, and she leaned towards him and buried her face against his chest. Lee held her to him, and then he clasped her shoulders and drew back.

'I want to make love to you. But this—this damned chair. . . My legs. . .' He swallowed drily. 'It would be no good, no good for either of us. And I—I think we should stop now, before we both—before I. . .' He paused. 'I'm very grateful to you, Danielle. But. . .'

Grateful. He was grateful. Was that why he'd been kissing her with such passion? Because he was grateful?

Somehow, she managed to smile as she rose slowly to her feet. 'You don't have to explain,' she said, walking quickly towards the fireplace. 'Anyway, it's late,' she said as she picked up a poker and bent to the hearth. 'I think we should call it a night, don't you?' He didn't answer, which seemed answer enough, and she put the poker aside and straightened up. Taking a deep breath, she turned to face him again. 'Can I get you anything before I go up? Hot chocolate? Tea?'

Lee's eyes were fixed on her face. 'Danielle. What is it?'

Her lips trembled with the effort to keep the smile on her face. 'Nothing,' she said, and she stretched her mouth into a smile so wide she was afraid it was a grimace. 'Nothing, honestly. I'm just—I'm tired. It—it's been a long day.'

He reached out as she walked past him. His hand curled around hers, his fingers warm and filled with strength.

'Danielle.' His voice was low. 'Thank you for everything.'

'Please,' she whispered. 'Don't thank me. It's not——'

'All those things you said tonight—I know it wasn't easy. I just want you to know I'm—I'm grateful.'

Grateful. There was that ugly, terrible word again. He was grateful.

'Danielle?' She looked down at him, and he smiled. Gently, he pulled her down to him, and his lips brushed softly against hers. 'Goodnight,' he whispered.

She watched as he wheeled his chair from the room. For the first time in weeks, his shoulders were set squarely and his head was high. She had done that for him, she thought, and the realisation sent a thrill of happiness through her. A smile curved across her lips, but it faded quickly away.

She had helped him find himself, and he was grateful to her for what she'd done. But it wasn't Lee's gratitude she wanted.

What she wanted was his love.

CHAPTER NINE

WHEN had she fallen in love with Lee? As dawn tinged the whitewashed stone walls of Danielle's bedroom with pink, she tried to make sense of her tumbling emotions. She hadn't fallen in love with him tonight, she knew that. She had loved him for a long time. For weeks. She had loved him even before the night of the accident.

Sighing, she rolled over on her stomach and buried her face in the pillow. That was why she'd locked herself away here, with him. What kind of foolishness had kept her blind to the truth for so long?

No. Not foolishness. It was self-protection. She hadn't dared let herself know what she felt for Lee because it was hopeless to love him, and she had known that instinctively. All the things that made Lee Bradford the man he was were things so far outside her realm of experience that the idea of their being together was almost laughable.

She was, just as he'd said from the beginning, a farm girl, if not in fact, then certainly in spirit. And he—he was a man who needed the excitement and glitter of a world she'd never even imagined, a world populated by women as beautiful and sophisticated as Valerie.

Danielle sat up and pushed aside the bedcovers. It would have been nice to have gone on pretending just a little while longer, she thought, wrapping her arms around her knees. But Lee had taken her in his arms in an act that was as much gratitude as desire, and that had forced her to face the truth.

She closed her eyes and nestled her cheek against her

upthrust knees. She had told Eddie the truth, too, and in almost the same way.

'I like you very much,' she'd said gently. 'And I'm grateful for your friendship, Eddie. But I don't love you the way you love me. I doubt if I ever will.'

The memory sent a knife-blade of pain into her heart. Poor Eddie. For the very first time, she understood how he must have felt. He'd loved her and known there had been no future to it, just as she knew there was no future in her love for Lee.

The only difference was that she hadn't told Lee she loved him. Thank God for small favours, she thought with a bitter smile. At least she hadn't bared her soul to him completely.

A soft twitter of birdsong rose on the early-morning air. Danielle swung her legs to the floor, walked to the window, and pushed the shutters wide open. The sun was halfway up the sky, fiery and beautiful in its ascent. The air was sweet with lavender, and as warm as blood even though it was still early in the morning.

The world lay soft and new all around her. It was a beautiful morning, the kind on which anything seemed possible. Well, she thought with a wry smile, almost anything. If Lee kept the promise he'd made last night, if the night hadn't plunged him back to the dark despair of the past weeks, she could help him begin to get well.

It wouldn't be the same as having his love. But it would, at least, fill her aching heart with some warmth.

The house lay silent around her as she tiptoed down the stairs. The door to Lee's room was partly open, but she knew he'd be asleep. He never rose until the sun was high; she thought, sometimes, it was just a way he used to shorten the day.

Her nose wrinkled as she headed for the kitchen. The air was scented with coffee. Had she forgotten to unplug the electric coffee-maker last night? It didn't seem likely, but you never knew.

'Good morning.'

Danielle gasped and clapped her hand to her heart. Lee was seated on the far side of the kitchen, smiling at her over the rim of a coffee-cup.

'My God,' she said with a little laugh, 'you scared the life out of me.'

'Sorry. I guess I should have called out when I heard your footsteps.' He swivelled his chair towards the open french doors that led to the terrace. 'But I was watching the birds in the garden. What are they? Sparrows?'

She looked past him at a flock of tiny brown birds busily pecking away at the soil.

'I think so. But I don't know what you call them in French.'

Lee glanced back at her. 'Did you do all that?'

'All what?' He gestured at the neat rows of herbs and flowers, and she smiled. 'The weeding? Is that what you mean?'

'It looks as if you worked a miracle out there.'

Danielle laughed. 'No miracles. Just lots of elbow-grease.'

He leaned forward in his chair. 'Are those roses I see along the back wall?'

'Yes. Wild ones, I think. They'd have to be, to have survived in that jungle.'

Lee smiled. 'Anything would survive, with you nurturing it.'

Their eyes met. After a moment, she looked away. 'Is that—is that coffee I smell?'

He grinned and wheeled towards the counter. 'Yup. Want some?'

'Yes, please.'

She watched as he poured a cup for her and then refilled his own. Making coffee was such a simple thing, she thought. It was ridiculous to feel this pleased about it. But for Lee, it was a milestone. In the weeks they'd been here, he hadn't so much as boiled water. It was as if he'd held himself aloof from even the smallest part of his recovery.

She smiled as she took the cup of coffee from him. 'Mmm,' she said, taking a deep breath, 'that really does smell wonderful.'

Almost as wonderful as he looked. He was wearing an old grey sweatshirt with the sleeves cut off. A faded line of dancing sparkplugs high-kicked across his chest. His dark hair curled damply at the nape of his neck. He'd showered, she thought, using the hand-held spray in his bathroom. It had to be a clumsy procedure, but Lee had refused her help from the start—which was just as well, she thought now. She could never run her hands over his water-slicked skin. . .

'Don't you like it?' Lee asked. Danielle stared at him blankly. 'The coffee,' he said. 'You had such a funny look on your face.'

She shook her head. 'I—I was thinking of something else.' She blew on the hot liquid, then took a sip. 'The coffee's perfect.'

Lee grinned. 'Coffee's one of the few things I can do in a kitchen. It's probably because all you need to succeed is water, a measuring scoop, and some grounds.'

She smiled back. 'You're not one of those men who loves making exotic casseroles, then?'

'I'm not one of those men who's ever had a kitchen,' he said with a little smile. 'Life on the racing circuit's lived in hotel rooms.'

Another milestone, Danielle thought, trying not to show her surprise. Lee hadn't mentioned racing since the day Bonet had explained the severity of his injuries.

'And away from the circuit?'

He shrugged as he spooned sugar into his coffee. 'I've

an apartment in New York and a little place in Switzerland.' He laughed softly. 'And maid service in both.'

Danielle pulled out a chair and sat down at the table. 'New York and Switzerland, hmm? Sounds nice.'

Lee nodded. 'Yeah. It is. The New York apartment overlooks Central Park. And the Swiss cabin is just outside Davos; I go there to ski whenever I. . .'

His smile faded and Danielle's heart went out to him. But something warned her against offering comfort. He would have to find his own way, she thought, and there was a new set to his jaw that assured her he would. He waited a few seconds, and then he cleared his throat.

'So,' he said briskly, 'did you sleep well?'

'Fine,' she said, lying glibly. 'And you?'

He hesitated, and then he shook his head. 'No. Not very.'

'Were you ill? You should have called me, Lee. I'd have——'

'I wasn't sick, Danielle.'

'Oh.' She gave him a quick smile. 'I thought——'

'I spent the night thinking about what an impossible son of a bitch I've been.'

'Lee. . .'

'I was a bastard,' he said. 'Right from day one.'

Her smile warmed a little. 'Well, if you insist.'

Lee grinned, and then his expression sobered. 'You must have known you were signing on for trouble—and yet you did it anyway.'

'I told you, we were helping each other. I needed a job, and——'

'Why did you stay? I mean, no one would have taken all the garbage I've handed out the past weeks.'

Because I love you, she thought.

The words came so swiftly that she was afraid she'd said them aloud. But Lee was still watching her with that same careful, polite smile. Danielle pushed back her chair and got to her feet.

'I admit, I came close to saying *au revoir* a couple of times,' she said with a quick smile. 'But I figured, a deal's a deal.'

'What about Val?'

She looked at him. 'Val?'

'Have you heard from her at all?' His voice was flat.

There'd been one postcard. 'Busy, busy, busy,' Val had scrawled, 'Love to Lee.' But she couldn't tell him that. That he'd asked about Val at all was a sure sign he was on the mend.

Danielle turned away and busied herself at the sink. 'Yes,' she said brightly. 'She wrote several times. I—I guess I should have saved the letters. She says she's working hard. And—and she sent you all her love.'

Silence fell between them, and then Lee cleared his throat. 'Look, about what happened last night. . .'

Danielle closed her eyes. 'We just—we got carried away, that's all. I mean, we were both upset, and—and. . .' She lifted her shoulders in a helpless shrug. 'What you said last night, about—about gratitude—made sense. So—so let's not talk about it any more, all right?'

Bird-calls filled the room, and then Lee let out his breath. 'All right.'

The room grew silent again. Finally, Danielle turned to him and smiled.

'What would you like to do today? I thought we'd have lunch on the terrace. And for dinner tonight, I'll——'

Lee laughed, and the sound of it scattered the awkwardness that had drifted into the room a moment ago.

'What are you trying to do to me, lady?' he demanded. 'I eat and I sleep, and then I eat some more. If I'm not careful, I'm going to turn into a mountain.'

Danielle smiled. 'A beached whale, hmm?'

He chuckled softly. 'You got it. I don't get any exercise—except forking food into my face. By the time Bonet springs me from this chair, I'm going to weigh five hundred pounds.'

'I don't think Weight Watchers has made it to Provence yet. They'd probably shoot me if I drove into Grasse and tried to buy low-calorie bread.'

'Would you rather watch me turn into old Moby Dick?'

She grinned at him. 'OK, you've convinced me. Tell you what. I'll go into town and buy some tins of tuna and whatever else I can find that. . .' Her eyebrows rose when she saw the look on Lee's face. 'No good?'

'This whale's lived on tuna long enough to have decided it's something to be eaten only on pain of death,' he said with a dramatic shudder.

Danielle leaned back against the counter. 'Somehow,' she said, folding her arms across her chest, 'I doubt that.'

'They asked me to write a cookbook,' he said, straight-faced. '*Bradford's Ten Thousand and One Ways to Serve Tuna*, from *à la* king to zabaglione.'

'Tuna zabaglione? God, I hope not.'

He smiled. 'I've probably opened more tins of tuna than any man should in an entire lifetime.'

'OK, I'll ask the obvious question. Why?'

He took a sip of coffee and shrugged as he swallowed it down. 'Tinned tuna is cheap, nutritious, easy to lug around—it's the perfect food for a guy on the road with no bucks in his pockets.' He looked at her as he put his cup down on the table. 'Which just happens to be a rather accurate description of me, a couple of eons ago. Every dime I could scrape together was in my first real car.'

'Your first *real* car?'

Lee grinned reflectively. 'Yes. A '59 Chevy, candy-apple red, with a three hundred and fifty-cc mill and Holly carbs. You should have seen. . .' Her blank looked stopped him. 'It was a racer. And I bounced from county fair to dirt track and back again, with side trips to God knows where and I-wouldn't-go-there-on-a-bet.'

Racing. He was talking about racing again.

'And that's how you started?' she asked softly.

Lee nodded. 'It's how most racing drivers start. And it's costly. Not as costly as Formula One, of course.'

'Is it very expensive to field a Formula One car?'

He laughed. 'How's ten million dollars a year sound, Danielle?'

Her eyes rounded in shock. 'For one car? I don't believe it!'

'For a car and a team. You've got to remember, Formula Ones are the most sophisticated racing machines in the world. And it takes a dozen people you don't see to make the car a winner. Mechanics, engineers, a team manager. . .' He smiled. 'All to make a guy like me look good.'

You don't need anything to make you look good, she thought.

Colour rose to Danielle's cheeks. What was the matter with her? Any minute now, she was going to say something thoughtless, and the what would happen to this new, wonderful friendship between them? She'd learned something from her relationship with Eddie: she knew what happened when one person loved and the other didn't. It put a burden on the one who didn't, it weighed like a stone.

Danielle nodded wisely. 'I never knew that.'

'Most people don't. The driver is the high-profile guy, the one who gets all the glory.'

She touched her tongue to her lips. 'Then—then you

wouldn't hate taking some other part in the team? The manager, say, or. . .'

Lee smiled gently. 'Ah, the lady's brain is whirring into high gear. If you're asking me, could I live without driving, the answer is yes, I could.' He took a deep breath. 'But if you're asking me, am I ready to give it up, the answer is no, not yet.' His eyes met hers. 'I meant what I told Bonet, you know. He's not God.'

Danielle's smile dimmed. 'But he said——'

'I know what he said. But he's never been a driver. It takes as much guts and skill as it takes muscle and bone.' His eyes drilled into her. 'Do you understand what I'm saying?'

Danielle ran her tongue over her lips. 'Yes. And—and I hope you're right. I just don't think you should—I mean, if you have expectations that don't—that may not work out. . .'

'Danielle, listen to me. I've always known I'd have to stop racing some day. Hell, everybody knows that, you think about it after a bad race or a crash—you think about it after a good race, too. You wonder how many more you have left in you.' He rolled his chair towards her and took her hand in his. 'To walk away from racing is different from being wheeled away from it in a bloody chair. Do you understand?'

She looked at him and nodded her head. 'Yes.'

Lee's hand tightened on hers. 'Last night, I promised a certain young woman I'd fight back. And I will.'

'I didn't mean——'

'I know you didn't. And I'm not building castles in the air, I promise. But there's no point in trying if you don't aim as high as you can. Right?'

She looked at him helplessly, and then she nodded. 'I guess.'

He grinned. 'Well, then, how about starting? You promised to help me, remember?'

Danielle smiled. 'Of course. Just tell me how.'

His smile was smug. 'Drive me to Grasse.'

'To Grasse?' she repeated, staring at him. He might as well have said the moon, she thought, remembering how much effort it had taken only yesterday to convince him to so much as go out on the terrace.

Lee laughed. 'You should see the look on your face, farm girl.' This time, the teasing name brought a smile to her lips, although she felt a catch in her heart. 'Yes. To Grasse. Can you do that for me?'

'I'll do anything for you,' she said softly, and then she tugged her hand free of his and turned away before he could read the whole truth of what she'd said in her eyes.

Lee whistled through his teeth and beat a light rhythm on the dashboard as the road unrolled before them. Danielle glanced over at him and smiled to herself. He looked wonderful, she thought. He was glowing with vitality. And he was so handsome. So. . .

Lee turned towards her. 'What are you thinking?'

Colour flooded her cheeks and she looked quickly back to the road. 'Nothing,' she said, staring straight ahead.

He smiled. 'Then why are you blushing?'

'I am not blushing. I was—I was just thinking that you look—you look very well. Healthy, I mean. You know.'

'Debonair. Sophisticated. Are those the words you're looking for?'

Her eyebrows rose. 'It must be hard to be so modest,' she said, trying to look stern.

He laughed as he lay his head back. 'It must be the sandal,' he said, tilting his toes so that the leather thong slapped against the floorboard. 'Women can't resist a man with only one shoe. Brings out their mothering instincts.'

She looked at him in surprise. Was he really joking about his legs? This was definitely a day of milestones, she thought, and her heart rose to her throat. But she knew enough to keep her response light, to match his.

'I wouldn't have thought you knew much about women's maternal instincts.'

Lee turned his head towards her. 'Women are one of the things that happen to a racer,' he said, after a minute. 'There are some who are attracted to the glitter or the danger—I'm not certain what draws them.' He paused. 'But they're there, and they're available. And racers—men like me—sometimes end up treating them the same as we do other perks. Hell, you say to yourself, if they're here, why pass them by?'

Danielle nodded, hating those unseen and unknown women with a burning ferocity that she hid with a casual smile. 'Sort of like being turned loose in a candy store, hmm?'

He laughed. 'Yes, I suppose it is.' His laughter faded. 'They don't mean anything, though. I mean, women are just—they're just women. I'm not proud to admit it, but sometimes I can't even remember their names.'

Her hands tightened on the steering-wheel. She knew what he was doing. This was a left-handed kind of compliment; he was telling her that their friendship rose above the sexual, reminding her that what had happened last night would not happen again.

'So much for you and women's maternal instincts,' she said lightly.

Lee smiled. 'I know it must come as a surprise,' he said, 'but even I have a mother.'

Danielle felt the tension begin to leave her. 'What's she like? No, don't tell me. She probably has the disposition of a saint.'

'To have tolerated me, you mean?' He laughed. 'My

Dad's the one that gave her the tough time, not me. At least I always knew what it was I wanted.'

'And your father didn't?'

Lee shook his head. 'He was an automobile mechanic when they met. By the time I was born, he ran an auto-parts store. That lasted a year or two, until he got bored and decided it was time for a change. So he went to work for a car dealership.'

Danielle smiled. 'So that's how you come by your love of cars.'

He nodded. 'I suppose. Funny, though, the one thing he never wanted was the thing I always did.'

'Racing, you mean.'

'Yes. I built my first go-kart when I was ten, pieced together my first souped-up old Pontiac when I was fourteen——'

'Fourteen?' She glanced at him, eyebrows arched. 'Where can you get a driver's licence at fourteen?'

Lee grinned. 'No place I know of, certainly not San Diego, where I grew up. What I did was put the car together, then conned a guy I knew to drive us to a place out in the hills. Then I got behind the wheel and put the pedal to the metal. . .' He shook his head. 'God, the dumb things kids do.'

Danielle flexed her fingers on the wheel. 'And you never got caught?'

'Nope. Never even came close. As soon as I was old enough, I began to enter dirt-track competitions. Small stuff, but it was enough so I began to learn and make contacts. My father staked me the money I needed to buy a decent car, but I had to make my own living expenses.'

She laughed softly. 'Enter tinned tuna,' she said.

Lee laughed, too. 'Exactly. With enough wins, it was possible to get a ride in Formula Three, then move up to Two——'

'What's that?'

'Racing categories, like One, but with smaller engines and lighter cars.' He looked at her and smiled. 'What about you, farm girl? What's your life like?'

She shrugged her shoulders. 'Dull, dull, dull. I went to college when Val went off to New York.' She smiled slightly. 'She used to send home these terrific letters about auditions and modelling shoots, and I'd read them in between cramming for exams.'

'And now you teach French, hmm?' Danielle nodded. 'To high school kids?' She nodded again. 'But you don't like it very much.'

Danielle looked at him in surprise. 'I do like it. A lot. Where did you get that idea?'

'You said teaching was dull.'

'Well, no, I didn't mean that, exactly. I just meant—I meant that what I do is dull, compared to—well, to what Val does.'

'Don't compare yourself to Val,' Lee said quickly.

A bitter taste filled her mouth. 'No,' she said softly, 'I suppose I shouldn't.'

He put his head back against the seat and stared out the window. 'You're not anything like her. She does outrageous things, but people—men—are willing to turn a blind eye. But you. . .'

A horn beeped sharply behind them, and Danielle looked into her mirror.

'Look,' she said. 'We're here, in Grasse. I'll have to find a place to park.'

Lee nodded. 'OK. I'll start looking.'

'Good idea,' she said brightly.

It was much better to look for a place to park than to listen to Lee tell her what she already knew.

Val—beautiful, sexy Val—had turned her back on him when he'd needed her most. But she was still very much a part of his life.

CHAPTER TEN

DANIELLE had heard as much speculation as anyone about the mysterious connection between mind and body. Ginny had once gone to St Louis for a weekend course in meditation. Afterwards, she'd talked, rather mysteriously, of bio-feedback and the art of funnelling one's energies into oneself.

'You can lower your blood-pressure and cure headaches and——'

'I'll bet.' Danielle's expression had been absolutely innocent. 'How's it on hangnails and adolescent acne?'

'It's not a joking matter,' Ginny had said with indignation. The friends' eyes had met, and a smile had flickered on Ginny's face. 'OK, I know it sounds funny. . .'

'Who taught this class, anyway? A seventies leftover wearing a long white robe?'

'He's not. Maharishi Levine is. . .' The women's eyes had met again, and Ginny had giggled. 'Anyway, his robe was blue.'

The women had burst into laughter. In the end, Ginny had wiped her eyes and sighed.

'Well, it was an interesting lecture,' she'd said. 'Better than another weekend spent doing laundry, anyhow.'

Now, watching Lee take command of his life again, Danielle began to wonder if she didn't owe Ginny's maharishi an apology. She could almost see Lee changing in front of her eyes, from a man grown passive in the face of adversity to one determined to mould his own future.

If it was at all possible to will yourself well, Lee would

do it. Their first stop in Grasse was at a chemist, where he plucked bottles of vitamins and protein supplements from the shelves.

'Kelpweed tablets?' Danielle said, shuddering as she peered over his shoulder.

Lee gave her a grim smile. 'If you think they sound bad, you ought to taste them,' he said, adding a second bottle to the first.

Out on the street again, he frowned as he peered at the shopfronts. 'There has to be a sporting-goods shop somewhere. Do you see one?'

'Yes. There's one at the corner. But——'

'Let's go, then,' he said. The muscles in his upper arms bulged as he wheeled his chair quickly up the street.

What could a man confined as Lee was need in a shop whose windows were filled with tennis rackets, golf-clubs, and scuba gear?

'Weights,' he said, as if he'd heard the unspoken question. 'Wrist weights and dumb-bells. Can you translate for me, please?'

She did, and a short time later the shopkeeper deposited an impressively heavy box into the boot of the car.

'What's next?' Danielle asked, smiling at him.

He grinned back. 'Lunch. I've worked up an appetite just thinking about using those weights.'

They lunched on a quiet terrace under the leafy branches of a flowering tree. Lee waved away the menus and ordered for them both with an easy assurance that bordered on arrogance. But it filled her heart with pleasure; the old Lee Bradford was back, she thought.

'*Soupe de poissons*,' he told the waiter. '*Et un demi de Château Simone blanc, s'il vous plaît.*'

Danielle put her elbows on the table, propped her chin in her hands, and smiled. 'Fish soup and a half-bottle of white wine, huh? I thought you didn't speak French.'

Lee laughed. 'What I speak is "menu". I've been on the circuit for years. I can get myself fed in any language where there's ever been a Grand Prix.' He leaned towards her. 'The fish soup's a speciality here—assuming you like garlic.'

Daniellc smiled. 'Garlic's one of my secret vices.'

He smiled in return. 'I should have known you'd be a woman of impeccable tastes.' The waiter arrived with two huge bowls of soup and a basket of hot, crusty bread. 'Come on,' Lee urged, 'eat up. You'll need your strength—we have lots of shopping left to do.'

They stopped at a toyshop next. 'Here we go,' Lee said cheerfully. 'Monopoly. Terrific!'

Danielle eyed the game warily. 'Well, yes. But it's the French version.'

He grinned at her. 'Yes, but there's a method to my madness, *mademoiselle*. Besides, I can beat you, hands down, no matter what the names of the streets and utilities.'

'Such modesty, *monsieur*,' she said archly.

Lee sighed. 'I just happen to be a world-class Monopoly player.'

Danielle laughed softly. 'I'm pretty good myself, pal.'

'Yeah?'

'Yeah,' she said, her eyes twinkling.

He smiled. 'We'll see. As for the French—I thought you might teach me the language while we play. How does that sound?'

The simple request filled her with joy. 'It sounds fine,' she said. 'I'd like that.'

At a bookshop around the corner, Lee bought English-language newspapers and magazines, and whatever books he could find on sports-related injuries and the men and women who'd suffered them. Two were in English, but the rest were in French.

'Would it be an imposition to ask you to read these to me?' he asked.

'No,' she said softly, 'not at all.'

Then he wheeled his chair to a stop beside a rack of paperback novels. 'What do you like?' he asked Danielle. 'Romances? Mysteries? Histories?'

She smiled at him. 'Mysteries. I've always promised myself that some day I'd buy every John MacDonald novel ever published and——'

'Hold out your hands,' he said.

When she did, he stacked a load of the MacDonald paperbacks into her arms.

'Lee.' She stared from the books to him. 'What are you——'

'It's summer vacation, teacher,' he said, smiling. 'You might as well relax and enjoy it.'

In a little gourmet shop tucked away on a quiet street, Lee filled a straw basket with tins of caviare and anchovies, crackers, cheeses, chocolates, and bottles of wine.

'We'll never eat all that,' Danielle insisted, but he waved away her protests.

'It's for cocktail hour.'

'But we don't have a——'

'Then it's time we did,' he said, adding a tin of cashew nuts to the basket. 'Besides, I'm going to have to keep my calories up once I start my exercise programme.'

He started that programme the very next day. The intensity of it at first astonished and then terrified her. Lee worked out twice a day, morning and evening, with the weights he'd bought in Grasse. The first time she heard him grunting and panting out on the terrace, Danielle raced outside, certain he'd fallen out of his chair.

But he hadn't. He was sitting shirtless under the relentless Provence sun, hoisting the dumb-bells high over his head. Muscles bulged in his forearms as sweat streamed down his body.

'Hi,' he gasped. 'Come to watch the torture session?'

That was exactly what it looked like. 'It's so hot out here,' Danielle said, watching as he strained. 'Why don't you work inside?'

He grunted. 'Sweating's good for you.'

Danielle laughed. 'That's silly.'

Lee grinned as he picked up the pace of the lifts. 'Maybe I just like the feel of the sun.'

Her smile faded. Maybe he did. His tanned skin was slick with sweat. His hair was damp, too, where it curled along the nape of his neck. Drops of dampness glistened like diamonds in the dark mat of hair on his chest. Her gaze slid lower, to the ridged muscles in his abdomen, and suddenly she felt a swelling heat move within her veins.

'Well, then,' she said with false brightness, 'have a good time.'

She fled to the safety of the garden where she plunged her hands into the soil, weeding the gangly plants with feverish determination.

Lee's laughter followed after her. 'Can't stand watching a guy suffer, hmm?' he called.

She waved, as if in agreement, which was much safer than letting him suspect there might be a deeper reason.

The simple truth was that watching Lee lift weights, body gleaming under the blazing sun, took her breath away. He was beautiful, as beautiful as any of the ancient Roman statues she'd seen in the ruins that dotted the hills above Nice. She ached to feel his arms around her, to feel the touch of his mouth against hers.

The depth of her need frightened her. It frightened her even more that Lee might read her desire in her eyes. He had made his feelings clear. The last thing she wanted was to hear him explain his gratitude to her again.

Twice they drove to Nice so that Dr Bonet could examine Lee's legs. On the second visit, the surgeon exchanged Lee's knee brace for one far lighter and smaller, and told him he could start using crutches.

'Not all the time,' Bonet warned. 'You must not put too much strain on yourself just yet.'

Lee assured the doctor he would not overdo it. But Danielle saw the set to his jaw, and she knew that the wheelchair was in its last days.

She almost said something when she saw the new routines he added to his daily work-outs. They were 'curls', he said, to strengthen his arm muscles so he would not tire on the crutches. A pulsing vein stood out on his forehead; he was pushing himself too fast, she thought—but the look in his eyes silenced her. It was useless to argue with that kind of determination.

But when she found him stretched flat on his back on the terrace floor, his face contorted in a rictus of agony as he lifted his left leg into the air, held it aloft for a slow count of ten, then lowered it again, Danielle decided it was time to speak out.

'What are you trying to do to yourself, Lee Bradford?' she demanded pushing open the french doors and stalking towards him. 'That knee. . .'

But he wasn't listening. He was lifting his leg again, counting softly in agonised gasps while the sweat poured down his face. His leg trembled with exhaustion when he lowered it.

'Lee, for God's sake.' Her voice lost all its anger. 'Please—you'll hurt yourself. You'll tear the ligament again or——'

'I know what I'm doing,' he panted. 'We read all those books together, remember? No pain, no gain. And I'm not new to this anyway. I've had injuries before.'

She stared at his leg, at the vivid red scar that slashed across the kneecap.

'But not like this,' she said softly.

Lee looked at her. 'No,' he said after a pause, 'not like ths. But I've come back each time, and I'm damned well going to again.'

And then he grunted and raised his leg again. 'One. Two. Three. . .'

Danielle watched for a few seconds, then turned and went into the cottage. His dedication was hard to fault. And, even though it sometimes looked as if he was going to hurt himself, he seemed to know what he was doing. He'd made incredible progress the past few weeks: his body, bronzed from the sun, was powerful and healthy.

The truth was, it wasn't really his body she was concerned about. It was his spirit.

Lee was determined to recover fully, to return to the life he loved. What if he couldn't? What if Bonet had been right, and his racing days were behind him? Would he be strong enough to accept that? Or would he plunge into a despair worse than the one he'd already suffered?

One lazy afternoon, they drove into the hills with a picnic lunch. Danielle waited until Lee was relaxed, lying back on the grass and gazing up at the clouds drifting slowly overhead, and then she cleared her throat.

'Lee? Have you—have you thought about—about what you'll do when the cast comes off?'

He looked at her. 'Bathe my damned leg,' he said drily. 'Do you know what it's like not to——'

She smiled unsteadily. 'That's not really what I meant.'

He turned away and stared at the sky again. 'I know what you meant, Danielle.' Slowly, carefully, he rolled to his side, then fought his way upright. 'And I think you know the answer,' he said, grasping his crutches. 'I'm going to race again. My cast comes off in two days.

There'll be enough time between then and the Italian Grand Prix so I can join my team and get ready.'

Danielle rose and walked alongside him towards the car. 'Are you—are you sure?'

Lee stopped and swung towards her. 'Sure of what?' His voice was dangerously soft. 'Sure I can make the Grand Prix in time, or that I can race at all?'

'Lee, please understand. I'm not trying to dampen things. It's just that I——'

'I told you before, walking away from racing is one thing. Crawling away is another. You of all people should understand that.'

'I don't, though. Is it—is it getting another job that worries you? You told me yourself how many people it takes to field a race car. . .'

He smiled at her. 'I'm not worried about a job at all,' he said gently. 'Sure, I'd want something to do with the rest of my life. Hell, I'm not a man who can sit around and watch daisies grow. But I don't need money. I've made a lot racing, more than I ever imagined.'

'Then why. . .?'

Lee's smile vanished. 'Weren't you the one who talked about never quitting?'

'You're twisting my words, Lee. Admitting you can't do something isn't quitting, it's——'

'Let's not debate it, Danielle. When a man starts a new life, he wants to start it on his own terms.' His eyes darkened as they swept across her face. 'Do you see?'

Danielle shook her head. 'No, I don't. What does it matter——?'

His mouth narrowed. 'Nobody wants pity.' His eyes met hers, and for a moment she thought she saw a fiery light burning deep within them. But then he swung away and hobbled quickly to the car. 'It—it has to come because—because it's right.'

'Nobody would offer a man like you a job out of pity, Lee. You——'

For the first time in weeks, his temper snapped. 'Dammit,' he said, yanking open the car door, 'just drop the subject, OK?'

He was silent the rest of the day. Danielle hoped his mood would improve the next morning. But he was edgy at breakfast. She watched through the french doors as he worked out on the terrace. It was the kind of late August day Provence was known for: the sky was a perfect blue, the sun a blazing gold disc. Heat shimmered in waves from the terrace floor.

The hour devoted to Lee's weights came and went, and still he lifted and grunted. Danielle glanced at the clock. Fifteen minutes passed, then twenty. Finally, when she could see his skin beginning to pale beneath its bronze tan, when the athletic shirt he wore was a sodden mass of dark grey, she marched out of the cottage.

'All right,' she said quietly. 'That's enough.'

Lee didn't look at her. His arms rose and fell in unbroken rhythm.

'No-ho pa-hain,' he gasped, 'no-ho——'

'No gain,' she said, stepping in front of him. 'Yes. That's your story. Mine is that you're going to collapse if you push yourself much further. It must be a hundred degrees out here. And——'

'Go inside,' he panted. 'Go on. Just. . .'

She knew it would be pointless to try and snatch the weights from him. They were heavy and Lee was strong, a combination that would defeat her. Instead, she clasped his wrists in her hands.

His eyes narrowed. 'What the hell. . .?'

'Put down the weights,' she said, staring at him.

'Danielle, dammit——'

'Put them down, Lee.'

He glared at her, and then he shook free of her hands. 'All right,' he said, dropping the weights on the table, 'what's this all about?'

'Sanity, that's what it's all about.' Ignoring his protests, Danielle unlocked the brake and pushed his wheelchair through the doors and into the kitchen. 'Here,' she said, pouring him a glass of fruit juice.

'I don't want it. And I don't like being treated like a two-year-old.'

'Then don't behave like one.' She held the glass out to him again. 'Drink this before you collapse of heat exhaustion.'

Lee snatched the glass from her hand. 'I'm not even close,' he said angrily. 'I'm still sweating. If you have heat exhaustion, you don't——'

'Damn you, Lee Bradford, drink that juice before I force it down your throat.'

They stared at each other, and then a quick smile tilted across his mouth.

'You would, wouldn't you?' When she said nothing, he sighed. 'What the hell. If it makes the lady happy. . .'

She watched as he drank the cold liquid in one long series of swallows. When he was done, he wiped the back of his hand across his mouth and handed the glass back to her.

'Now get out of that shirt and towel off,' she said, tossing him a terry towel.

He yanked off his shirt and draped the towel over his shoulders. 'Satisfied?'

'No.' Her voice was grim. 'I want to know why you're doing this.'

'Doing what? Working out? I've been doing that every morning for the past——'

'Don't you dare patronise me,' she said sharply. 'You're killing yourself out there. You didn't say a word at breakfast, or at dinner last night.' Her eyes searched his. 'Lee,' she said, her voice suddenly soft, 'please—tell me what's wrong?'

There was a silence, and then he reached past her and grabbed his crutches from where they rested against the wall. 'Nothing,' he said, grunting as he hoisted himself up, then hobbled past her into the cool corridor. 'Does something have to be wrong for a man to——?'

'Don't do this,' she said, hurrying after him. 'I won't let you.'

Lee moved past her into the living-room and sank on to the sofa. 'I don't know what you're talking about,' he said, setting his crutches aside.

'I won't let you shut me out again,' she said. Her words were defiant, but her heart was hammering.

'Really?' His lips drew back from his teeth. 'And just what do you propose to do about it?'

Danielle drew a deep breath. 'I—I'll leave you here,' she said. 'I—I'll go out that door and drive to Nice.'

His eyes narrowed. 'Is that right?' he said in a soft, ominous voice.

She swallowed. 'Yes. If—if you crawl back inside yourself, I——'

She jumped as he slammed his hand against the arm of the sofa. 'That's not what I'm doing, dammit.'

Danielle knelt down beside him. 'Then what *are* you doing?'

He stared at her, his jaw clamped tightly shut. Then, when she had almost despaired of getting an answer, he puffed out his breath.

'Getting ready,' he said, his voice so soft she had to strain to hear it.

Danielle shook her head. 'I don't——'

'For my visit to Bonet tomorrow.' His eyes lifted to hers, and what she saw there made her heart stop. 'The cast comes off tomorrow. Have you forgotten?'

Had she forgotten? She didn't know whether she

wanted to laugh or cry. How could she have forgotten? It was all she thought about, worrying each time she looked at him that he would expect too much of himself when Bonet cut away the plaster shield, that he would want to be too strong too quickly.

Suddenly, she understood. He was afraid. And the only way he knew to handle that fear was to push his body—and his mind.

Danielle put her hand on his. 'Oh, Lee,' she whispered. 'Lee, it's going to be all right. You'll see.'

His hand caught hers tightly. 'Will it?' he said. 'That's what I keep telling myself. But——'

'Yes.' She leaned forward and put her other hand on his cheek. 'Yes,' she said again, turning his face to hers. 'Of course it will. You've come so far, Lee. You've done wonders.'

His eyes met hers. 'I spent all last night telling that to myself,' he said softly. He gave her a faint smile. 'By dawn, I had a pretty good argument going. "You'll collapse like a house of cards when you try to stand on your own," one part of me said, and the other snorted and said, hell, I'd be just fine.'

Danielle's eyes searched his. 'Why didn't you wake me?' she demanded. 'I'd have made us some tea, we could have talked. . .'

Lee smiled. 'I almost did. But. . .'

'But?'

His smile changed. He caught her hand and brought it to his lips. 'But—but what I needed—that kind of help—a man doesn't ask for,' he said, his breath warm and moist against her palm. He looked into her eyes. 'Do you understand?' he whispered.

She didn't, not right away, and then her heart turned over. Yes, she thought, staring at him, yes, she understood. Lee was a man who had spent his life in a dangerous, virile sport—and now, as he saw it, he had been reduced to something less than a man. It was how he'd felt at the beginning, just after the accident. He'd got over that during the past weeks, but now, with the moment of truth at hand, the terrible fear that had almost immobilised him had come back.

He needed a final proof of his strength, one that he could never doubt. He needed the most basic proof of all, the one only a woman could offer. That was why he'd been awake, thinking of her. She could move him past the final hurdle. She could take him into her arms, kiss away the darkness she saw in his eyes.

She could give him back his sense of self, and his masculinity. But what would happen to her when it was over? Could she face finding him and losing him all at once?

Tears rose in her eyes and glistened on her lashes.

'Danielle. I didn't mean to make you cry. I shouldn't have said anything.'

'It's not that,' she whispered brokenly. 'You—you don't understand.'

'I do.' He touched his hand to her hair. 'Forgive me, sweet. I shouldn't have. . .'

She lifted her face to his. 'There's nothing to forgive.'

He stared at her while time stood still. Then he groaned softly and his arms went around her as she knelt before him.

'Danielle,' he said softly. He drew her to him, and she sighed as his lips brushed hers. 'Come here,' he whispered. 'Just let me—let me hold you.'

Yes, she thought, just that. Surely there was no harm in offering him the comfort of her arms. She moved closer to him, her eyes closing as he lifted the hair from the nape of her neck and pressed his mouth to her skin. Her head fell back as he trailed soft kisses along the long column of her throat.

'Danielle,' he said, his voice thickening, 'just let me—let me. . .'

She moaned as his hand cupped her breast. She could feel her nipple hardening beneath his touch, her flesh swelling under the warmth of his palm.

A sob caught in her throat and she put her hands against his naked chest. His heart thudded beneath her fingertips. He was so beautiful, she thought, looking at him from beneath her lashes. Desire had darkened his eyes until they were midnight pools, hardened his mouth so that she longed to soften it with her lips.

He had been hers this summer—they had laughed together, fought together, worked together—and the summer was ending too soon. He was going to go back to his own world. She knew it, suddenly, knew it without question. His legs were going to be strong. It was what he wanted, what she wanted, too.

He would regain himself. And when he did, he would leave her. She would have nothing for the rest of her life but bitter-sweet memories of a summer spent in the hot sun with a man she would never forget.

Something dark and fierce stirred deep within her heart. If memories were all she'd have of Lee, then she would make the most of them. She would take what she could and tuck them away against the long, lonely years.

Sighing, she slid her hands up his chest to his shoulders, then to his neck. His flesh was warm and firm, as she had known it would be. She whispered his name softly, her eyes on his, and suddenly he gathered her to him so tightly that he stole her breath away. She could feel his power flowing into her, infusing her with blazing heat.

Her mouth parted to the thrust of his tongue, and Lee groaned softly as he tasted her. He whispered her name against her lips, and then he drew back and looked deep into her eyes. His fingers went to the top button of her shirtwaister dress, as they had that night so many weeks before. But this time there was no stopping. The first button opened, then the next, and finally her dress slipped from her shoulders and fell away.

'You're so beautiful,' Lee said thickly.

Danielle smiled. She felt beautiful at this moment. Lee's caresses, his kisses, had done that. And she felt powerful, filled with a witchcraft as old as time. She would be passion and desire, she would be Eve in the Garden of Eden, but in giving herself to him she would not be his undoing, she would be his strength. She would come to him in love, as she had dreamed of doing—as she never would again.

She smiled again, a smile that made Lee's breath catch in his throat.

'You're beautiful, too,' she said softly. Slowly, she eased the towel from his shoulders. She watched the play of emotion on his face as she ran her hands over his naked chest. 'I've dreamed of touching you,' she whispered.

His skin was hot as the Provence sun. It felt like silk to her questing fingers, silk laid over the hard musculature of his body. Whorls of hair matted his chest, and she closed her eyes as she explored the rough texture.

Lee cupped her face in his hands. 'Kiss me,' he said, and she lifted her mouth willingly to his. 'Yes,' he murmured against her lips, 'that's the way. Open to me, darling. Let me taste you.'

She moaned softly, returning kiss for kiss with an abandon she had never imagined possible. But when he opened the front clasp of her bra, her arms rose instinctively to cover her breasts.

'Don't hide yourself from me, Danielle,' he whispered. 'I want to see you. I've dreamed about seeing you.'

He caught hold of her wrists and slowly lowered her arms to her sides. She watched him from under drooping lashes as he gazed at her. The hunger in his face raised a quick flutter low in her belly. She held her breath as Lee lifted his hand and moved it slowly to her, then cried out as his fingers drifted lightly over her nipples.

'Do you like that?' he asked in a whisper that was fierce and tender all at once. He lifted her on to his lap, cradling her against him. Her eyes closed; she heard the rasp of his breath, then felt the warmth of it on her flesh as he bent towards her. His lips closed around her nipple and she cried out as he drew it into his mouth.

'Danielle,' he said softly. He clasped her shoulders and drew gently away. 'You'll have to help me.'

For a moment, she stared at him without comprehension. Then she smiled. 'Yes,' she whispered.

Together, they tugged off his denim cut-offs. Lee's body was powerful and perfect, beautiful in its maleness.

He took her into his arms again, kissing her more and more deeply as he crushed her against him. Once, she pressed inadvertently against his knee and she drew back, hissing her concern.

'Your poor legs,' she said.

Lee caught her shoulders. 'I don't want pity,' he said in a tight, angry voice.

She looked up at him. His face had gone dark. 'I only meant——'

'Let me worry about my legs,' he said.

His hands moved over her body, his callused fingertips stroking her thighs, her breasts, bringing life to her flesh. Heat bloomed like a flower in her loins.

Danielle sighed his name. Her hands moved over his face as they kissed. She had wanted to touch him for so long, she thought, she had ached to feel the heat of his hard body against hers, and now—and now. . .

She caught her breath as he clasped her waist and lifted her over him. 'Lee. How—how. . .?'

'Shh,' he whispered, his eyes on hers. 'Shh, sweet Danielle.'

'I can't,' she said. 'Please. . .'

He caught her mouth with his, his hands supporting and arranging her as she moved over him. Her hair fell around them like a cloud. He lowered her slowly on to his lap; she gasped as she felt the urgent press of him against her, felt the velvet warmth, the engorged power. Her body opened as the heat that had been building deep within her became his heat, invading her flesh.

Danielle cried out Lee's name as he thrust upwards and entered her.

'Yes,' he whispered. 'Yes, that's right, yes, sweet, yes.'

His hands clasped her hips. Together, like dancers finding their way to some new and wonderful music, they began to move.

She heard the moaning keen of her own voice, heard Lee's answering hoarse cry—and then the earth dropped away. She was soaring into the sun, and the radiance of the universe was all around her.

When she came back to the world, she was curled in Lee's arms. He kissed her lips, her throat, then drew her face to his chest.

'Are you all right, sweetheart?' he asked softly.

She didn't trust herself to speak. Her heart was too full. She nodded and touched her hand to his cheek.

He laughed gently. 'You see?' he whispered, smoothing the damp curls back from her forehead. 'Didn't I tell you not to worry about my legs?'

Even with her face safely buried against his chest, Danielle blushed. 'Are you sure I didn't hurt you? I—I didn't think we could. . .'

Lee smiled. 'I didn't think so, either. But we did.' His voice grew thick. 'And we will. Come with me to my room, Danielle. I want to lie down and hold you in my arms.'

'Lee,' she said, looking up at him, 'are you sure you. . .?'

His mouth brushed against hers. 'Come with me,' he said urgently.

Minutes later, lying beside him, wrapped in his arms, Danielle stopped thinking about his legs, about what lay ahead—about anything but the man she loved.

Reality only returned with dawn's first light, when she awoke again, as she had throughout the night, to Lee's kisses.

She felt him smile against her throat. 'What are you thinking?' she whispered.

He laughed softly. 'That the sawbones can do his worst this afternoon,' he said, touching her. 'I'm as ready for Bonet as I'll ever be.'

His words meant she had given him back the self-confidence he needed. They warmed her heart—and, at the same time, they broke it.

Soon, Lee Bradford would be lost to her forever.

CHAPTER ELEVEN

WHEN Danielle woke again, the bedroom blazed with sunlight. She was alone in Lee's bed—the bathroom door was shut, and she could hear the sound of running water coming from the hand-held shower.

She sat up, blinking as she caught a glimpse of herself in the mirror on the far wall. Her hair was a softly tangled cloud. Her mouth was swollen, still warm with Lee's kisses. And there was a faint bruise at the juncture of throat and shoulder.

A smile hovered on her lips. The signs of Lee's possession were on her body.

Her smile trembled, then fell away. How could she face him this morning? The long, sweet night had left her defenceless. She felt as if she were wearing her emotions on her sleeve—all he'd have to do to see the truth of her love was look at her.

What a fool she'd been to think she could carry this off.

She started as the sound of running water stopped. She couldn't face him. Not just yet. She needed time to get herself together. . . Quickly, she pushed back the blankets, then rose from the bed and raced across the room. Her bare feet were soundless wings flying up the slate steps. When she reached the safety of her own room, Danielle closed the door behind her and fell back against it.

She had already turned on the shower when she heard Lee call her name. She leaned against the door, heart pounding. Her pulse tripped when she heard the scrape of his crutches across the tile floor downstairs.

'Danielle?' he said again.

Huddled in silence, she waited. Time dragged until she heard him move off down the hall.

But she couldn't hide forever. She took as long as she could showering and dressing, until finally there was only a little time left until they had to leave for Nice and Lee's appointment with the doctor. Then, with only minutes to fill, Danielle made her way slowly down the stairs.

Lee was in the kitchen. He didn't see her; he was standing at the far side of the room, sipping a cup of coffee as he looked out at the garden. Her heart swelled. She longed to run into his arms, to kiss him and tell him she loved him. But she couldn't, she'd known that all along.

Unless. . . Her pulse quickened. She was too old for believing in miracles, yes. Still, the night in Lee's arms had been a miracle, hadn't it? Anything was possible. Anything——'

The jangling ring of the telephone made her jump. Who would call at this hour? she thought, glancing at the clock. Not Lee's team-mates or Wexler. It was probably the doctor's office, phoning to confirm his appointment.

Lee reached back and picked up the receiver. 'Bradford.' He listened for a moment, then shook his head. 'No,' he said softly, 'don't come here. I'll meet you in Nice. At one o'clock. Right. In that little café around the corner from—yes, that's the one. No. No, of course not. I'll be alone, Val. Monaco?' He laughed softly. 'Yes, I'm looking forward to it, too. And then Italy?'

Danielle fell back, stunned. Val? Lee was on the phone with Val? But—but Val hadn't called here all these weeks, she hadn't cared enough to. . .

Lee turned as he hung up the receiver. Their eyes met. There was a silence, and then he managed a forced smile.

'Hi. I thought the smell of coffee might get you moving.'

Her smile was as forced as his. 'Yes. It did.' She walked to the counter, poured herself some, and took a sip. 'That's good,' she said brightly, as if coffee were all that mattered this morning. Say something about the phone call, she thought. But the seconds ticked away, and finally she looked at him, her smile this time even more artificial than the last. 'That's the first time the phone's rung in days.'

Lee's eyes slipped from hers. 'Yes,' he said, turning his back to her. 'It was—er—it was Wexler. I—I called him last week and told him I'd be in Nice today, if there was any technical stuff he wanted to check with me.'

Danielle's throat tightened. 'Ah,' she said, 'Barney Wexler. Of course.'

'Yeah.' He glanced at her as he hobbled to the coffee-pot. 'Seems he's gone over-schedule on the film.' He paused. 'It turns out they haven't shot all the race footage yet. They want me to come to Monaco next week.'

'Is that so?' Was that crisp voice really hers? 'Well, I suppose if Bonet give you the go-ahead. . .'

'About Bonet,' he said quickly. 'I arranged for a taxi to Nice, Danielle. I—I have to see this through on my own.' He touched his tongue to his lips. 'I hope you understand.'

She turned away. There would not even be this day, then. Oh, Lee, she thought, Lee. . .

'You don't have to explain anything to me.' Her voice was rushed, the words almost slurred. 'Starting today, what you do is—is your own business.'

Lee's crutches scraped across the floor. He stopped just behind her and put one hand lightly on her shoulder.

'Danielle, I—I just want you to know that when Bonet takes off this cast, when I can get on with my life again. . .' He puffed out his breath. 'I'll never forget what you've done for me,' he said softly.

Tears trembled on her lashes and she blinked them away. 'I'm glad I could help,' she said, easing away from his grasp.

'You did more than "help". I don't know how I'd have got through the summer without you.'

'Well,' she said brightly, 'that makes two of us. Thanks to the deal we made, I——'

'What deal?'

She took a breath, then turned to face him with what she prayed was a smile pasted to her lips. 'You gave me a job when I needed one. And a place to stay.'

Lee smiled. 'Are we back to that?' he said, watching her closely. 'I didn't fall for that story the first time you tried it on me.' He took a step forward. 'Don't you think it's time you admitted the truth?'

Panic beat in her pulse. 'That is the truth. I. . .'

His smile tilted. 'Come on,' he said in a coaxing whisper. 'After last night, you can give me the satisfaction of hearing you say it.'

Danielle stared at him. Suddenly, that arrogant smile of his was back, spreading across his face like the return of an unwelcome guest. Her heart lurched. They had come full circle, she thought bitterly. The old Lee Bradford, in hiding these past few weeks, had returned.

His hand closed around the back of her head, his fingers moved softly along her nape, as they had last night, playing against her skin until her nerve-endings were all sensitised.

'Tell me,' he whispered.

Oh, God. What did he want from her now? She had already given everything. Everything but the little pride left to her—and not even he could take that away. It was the one great lesson of her life: some parts of yourself must never be for sale.

Think. Damn it, think! There must be something you can say, something you can tell him.

'Actually,' she said, her voice trembling, 'there was another reason. I never—I never told you about Eddie, did I?'

Lee's smile vanished. 'Eddie? Who the hell is Eddie?'

She faltered for a second. Suddenly, there was something dark in his face, something that frightened her.

'Well? I'm waiting. Who's Eddie?'

'He was—he was a man I knew.' She drew a steadying breath. 'He—he was killed in a car accident.'

Lee stared at her. 'Killed? In a. . .?'

Danielle nodded. 'Yes. I—I saw it happen. And that's why—that's why. . .'

Her voice faded away. Stupid, she thought, stupid! Why was she telling him this? Yes, she'd seen Eddie die, but it wasn't the reason she'd offered to help Lee. Her pathetic story was cheapening Eddie's memory, cheapening the love she felt for the man standing before her. She wanted to call back her words. But what could she substitute for them? What could she say that would leave her with a shred of dignity?

Lee's hand tightened on her. 'Is that the reason you collapsed the day of the stunt crash?'

She nodded. 'Yes.'

'And the reason you offered to help me? Because you—you hadn't got over this man's death?'

She caught her bottom lip between her teeth. 'It was—it was something like that.'

His face darkened until it was like a thundercloud. 'And is that the reason you slept with me last night?'

His thumb lay in the hollow of her throat, pressing lightly against her pulse.

'Must we talk about that? What happened was just—was just. . .'

'Answer me, dammit. Was there a ghost in that bed with us?'

She flinched at the rawness of his words. Say yes, she told herself, but she couldn't.

'No,' she said softly. 'That was—that was. . .' She fell silent.

'Was what?' His voice was ominously soft.

She couldn't lie. Not about this. In the end, all she could do was shake her head. 'It—it had nothing to do with Eddie,' she whispered. 'I did that—I did that for you.'

Lee's hand fell away from her. 'God,' he said softly, 'Val was right about you after all. You'll do anything, if you think somebody needs you.'

The colour drained from Danielle's cheeks. 'That's not true.'

His mouth twisted. 'You went to bed with me last night to give me the courage you thought I needed before my cast comes off today.'

'It—it wasn't the way you make it sound. I knew you needed to prove yourself. But. . .'

His face contorted with disgust, just as it had the night of the accident, the night he'd started to make love to her before he'd shoved her out of the car.

'My God.' He shook his head. 'I don't know whether to feel sorry for you or to. . .' He fell silent, and suddenly a car horn rent the fabric of the late-summer morning. Lee let out his breath, grasped his crutches tightly, and shoved past her. 'That's my taxi.'

Danielle stared as he swung towards the front door, and then she hurried after him.

'Lee? Will you—will you be back?'

He stopped and looked back at her. 'Yes. Just long enough to collect my things.' He stared at her, as if there was something more he wanted to say, and then he turned away quickly and swung down the steps. 'Goodbye, Danielle.'

She stood in the open doorway, watching as he made his way to the taxi. It started slowly, then bounced on to the narrow track that arrowed through the ancient olive grove, swaying from side to side as it picked up speed, vanishing at last in a cloud of hot Provençal dust.

Slowly, Danielle stepped inside the cottage and closed the door. Then, as if she had aged a century in the past minute, she made her way up the slate staircase to her room.

'Missouri in winter.' Ginny sighed, leaning her elbows on the window-sill as she peered out into the darkening sky. 'Somebody should write a poem about it.'

Danielle looked up from the ancient sewing-table she was refinishing and smiled. 'They can't. It's hard to find rhymes for snow, ice, and brrr!'

Her friend laughed as she turned around. 'Isn't that the truth?' She sighed again as she sank down on the carpet opposite Danielle. 'I guess you don't believe all that stuff about not being able to turn a sow's ear into a silk purse, hmm?'

Danielle eyed the table warily. 'Are you trying to tell me this thing still looks as if it should be firewood?'

'I'm afraid so, my friend.'

'Well, then,' Danielle said grimly, 'I'll just have to oil it harder.'

Ginny watched for a while, then yawned. 'Want to take in a movie tonight?'

'I don't think so, thanks.'

'Yeah, it's probably not a good idea. It's supposed to snow later, and you know that old car of mine.' She pursed her lips. 'Just think, Danielle—your aunt and uncle are baking in the Arizona sun while we freeze our buns off.'

Danielle pushed back her hair and smiled. 'Um-hmm.'

'What I wouldn't give to be someplace where the sun still knows how to shine.' Ginny sighed. 'I'll bet it's hot as blazes in Florida. Or Mexico. Or the Riviera.'

Danielle's head came up sharply. 'What's that supposed to mean?'

Her friend stared at her. 'Did I forget to say that in English? It means,' she said with deliberate slowness, 'I'll—bet—it's—hot—as—blazes—in. . .'

Danielle sighed and tossed the polishing rag aside. 'Sorry,' she said. 'I didn't mean to take your head off.'

Ginny's eyebrows rose delicately. 'Nothing terribly unusual in that, though. You take my head off each time I mention the Riviera, or Provence.'

'I don't. You're exaggerating. I simply——'

'Or last summer.' Ginny paused. 'Aren't you ever going to tell me what happened to you over there?'

'Nothing happened. I went to France, spent the summer, and came home. End of story.'

'*How I Spent My Summer Vacation*,' Ginny said, waggling her eyebrows. 'By Danielle Nichols. For goodness' sake, third-graders do better reports than that.'

Danielle picked up the polishing cloth again. 'What do you want? A day-by-day account?'

Her friend smiled. 'I'd be satisfied with an account of how it feels to spend the whole summer with Lee Bradford.'

Danielle's cheeks flushed. 'Come on, Ginny. That's not——'

'School started again five months ago. And I still haven't got a whole sentence out of you about that man—which strikes me as a little weird, my friend, considering that you lived with him for——'

'I didn't live with him. I just. . .'

'OK. Poor choice of words.' Ginny leaned forward.

'At least tell me what's he's like. Aside from gorgeous, I mean.'

'Honestly!' Danielle's tongue peeked out between her teeth as she bent over the table and rubbed at its surface. 'You've been locked away with teenagers too long. You're beginning to sound like them.'

Her friend blew out an exasperated breath. 'Look who's talking. I, at least, go out for an evening with one of our local eligibles.' She made a face. 'Which reminds me—Barry Arnold's taking me to dinner Saturday. His cousin is in from Detroit—he's a doctor or a dentist or something. How would you like to——?'

'No. I mean, I can't.'

'I know. You have to do something vital. Like wash your hair. Or defrost the fridge.' She watched as Danielle worked furiously at the old table. 'Or polish that stupid thing until your hands fall off.' Ginny leaned forward and touched her friend's arm. 'Hey,' she said softly, 'don't you think it's time we talked about it?'

Danielle frowned. 'I give up. Maybe I'll take this down to that little refinishing shop we passed last week. Remember? The one with the curly maple desk in the window? What the heck—how much can it cost?'

Ginny eyed her narrowly. 'Certainly not more than it costs to get a word out of you.'

For a moment, Danielle went on staring at the table. Then she sighed, tossed aside the cloth, and slumped back on her heels. 'OK,' she said. 'What do you want to know?'

Ginny looked at he. 'Only what you want to tell me.'

Danielle laughed. 'Come on, Gin, you have to be kidding. You've been after me and after me for months—and now that you've finally worn me down, you say you only want to hear what I want to tell you?' She blew a strand of hair from her face as she got to her feet. 'That's like the Grand Master of the Inquisition peeling somebody off the rack and saying, "Only tell me what you wish to confess, my son."'

Ginny smiled. 'OK, point taken.' She rose and followed Danielle to the kitchen. 'Look, all I'm trying to say, in my not so graceful way, is that I want to help you.'

'Well, you can. Set the table while I put together something to eat.'

'I've seen that look in your eyes,' Ginny said as she laid out silverware and napkins. 'You can't fool me.'

'What look?' Danielle yanked open the refrigerator door and peered inside. 'How does a grilled cheese sandwich sound?'

'Fine,' Ginny said, taking cups and saucers from the cupboard and setting them on the old-fashioned oak table. 'And you know what "look" I'm talking about.'

'Tea,' Danielle said briskly. 'Or coffee. Which?'

'Whichever. And I wish you'd stop trying to change the subject.'

'I'm not changing the subject. We are talking about a light supper. And I said——'

'We were talking about that look you get, the one I never saw on your face until you came back from Nice.' Ginny sank into a chair. 'How long have we been friends?'

Danielle smiled as she buttered thin slices of wholewheat bread, then layered on cheese. 'Long enough to know you're going to hate this sandwich. I'm sorry, Gin—I'm out of tomatoes. Can you survive?'

Ginny hissed out her breath. 'Sure,' she said after a pause. 'I can survive. Can you?'

There was sudden silence in the room. Then the women's eyes met.

'Yes,' Danielle said evenly. 'I can. And I will. Satisfied?'

Ginny smiled sadly. 'Surviving isn't what it's all about, my girl. These are the good years—hasn't anybody told you? We're young, we have all our own teeth—we're supposed to be out there, having fun.'

'Well, I am. I'm busy fixing up my house, I've got an honours French class to teach, I'm thinking of visiting Aunt Helen and Uncle John at Easter. . .'

'Speaking of the old folks,' Ginny said, 'how's Val?'

Danielle shrugged as she set the timer on the oven toaster. 'OK. I guess. Aunt Helen says she's back in LA, trying to break into TV.'

'You haven't heard from her since the summer, have you?'

'No. How do you want your tea? With——?'

'Danielle.' Ginny's voice was soft with concern. 'What happened in Provence?'

Back to the beginning, Danielle thought. Her hands shook as she poured boiling water into the teapot.

'I told you what happened. I worked on Val's film for a while. And then—and then. . .' She bit her lip. 'Would you believe I can't remember if you take milk or lemon?'

'And then you set up house with——'

'I didn't "set up house". I told you that.' The oven buzzed, and Danielle breathed a sigh of relief. 'Supper,' she said briskly, 'such as it is.'

She put the meal on the table. They ate in silence for a few minutes, and then Ginny cleared her throat. 'What's he like, this Lee Bradford? I mean, you can tell me that, can't you?'

Danielle shrugged. 'Like—like anybody else.'

'I saw his picture on the cover of *Newsweek*,' Ginny said flatly. 'He sure didn't look like anybody else to me.'

'He—he's handsome. OK? Is that what you want to hear?'

'Have you heard from him?'

'No.' Danielle patted her lips with her napkin, then

put it on the table. 'And I don't expect to. Now are you satisfied?'

'Are *you*?'

Danielle inhaled deeply. 'Listen,' she said softly, 'whatever you're thinking is way off base. I—I helped Lee Bradford out and he did the same for me. That's all that happened. Anything else is the product of an over-active imagination.'

'Really? I was here the other evening, remember? The TV was on, they were doing an interview with this Bradford guy. . .'

Danielle's eyes clouded. 'Yes. He's racing this week in Buenos Aires.'

'You had this look on your face that was enough to break my heart,' Ginny said gently.

'What look? I didn't——'

'The same one you're wearing now.'

Danielle stared at her friend and then she got to her feet and walked across the kitchen. 'I forgot the tea,' she said. 'Wasn't that silly?'

'He wasn't supposed to race again, was he? That was what *Newsweek* said.'

'It was what the doctor said, too. But Lee—Lee wouldn't let himself believe that. He—he worked hard at building himself up.' Her voice faded.

'And?' her friend prompted gently. 'What happened?'

'And it worked. He's won two Grands Prix since then, in Italy and Canada. The last time out, he broke the record for. . .' Danielle fell silent.

'Amazing,' Ginny said softly. 'You seem to have turned into a sports fan. I remember the days when I had to poke you in the ribs to remind you to cheer for the old home team.'

Danielle inhaled sharply. 'My goodness,' she said briskly, 'just look at the time. Ginny, you're going to have to forgive me. I have papers to grade, and I'll never get them done if I don't start now.'

Ginny stared at her friend, and then she sighed. 'Sure. I have to be running along anyway.' She pushed back her chair and got to her feet. 'Dan? If you let that cousin of yours get between you and that guy, if you let her take him away. . .'

The women's eyes met. 'It wasn't Val's fault, Ginny. Nobody took Lee away from me. I—I never had him. Nobody has a man like that. He—he belongs to himself. He. . .' Danielle put her hand to her mouth. Seconds passed, and then she swallowed. 'Go home, Ginny,' she said softly. 'I'll call you tomorrow.'

Moments later, she sank back against the wall as the front door swung shut. She would never let what had just happened happen again. Ginny had suspected something all these months, ever since she'd seen a red-eyed Danielle step off the plane from Nice. But she'd managed to parry her questions—until now.

Danielle sighed wearily as she walked slowly to the kitchen. The interview the other day, the one Ginny had caught her watching, had set her back. She had finally got herself to the point where she could sometimes manage an entire morning or afternoon without thinking about Lee. Never both, she thought with a trembling smile, and never, never a whole night.

But seeing him on the television screen, hearing his familiar voice, had changed all that. She'd lost ground, and she still hadn't recovered it.

With a sigh, she collected the few supper dishes and piled them in the sink. Was Ginny right? Would it help if she talked about Lee? She turned the spigot and hot water gushed into the sink. Maybe it would. But she couldn't do it. It wasn't as if she'd made a conscious decision not to discuss him or what he meant to her; it was something that went far deeper than that.

Memories were fragile things, like tiny figures fashioned of glass. She knew that better than anyone—the wispy images of the mother and father she'd loved and lost had faded over the years until now there were times when the remembered faces were just a little fuzzy in her mind.

Danielle closed her eyes. That wasn't going to happen this time. Her memories of Lee had to last forever. And they would, if she cherished them and didn't let them become topics for discussion and debate.

She knew Ginny thought that she'd fallen in love with Lee and lost him to Valerie. Danielle poured herself another cup of tea and carried it into the living-room. But it wasn't true—his liaison with her cousin hadn't lasted very long. Val had made the most of the chance to boast about it, though. There'd been a postcard soon after she'd arrived home, scrawled in Val's lazy hand.

'Lee's fit as a fiddle,' Val had written. 'I bought him a walnut and sterling cane—very classy. On to Italy for the Grand Prix. Wish you were here. Love, love, love—Val.'

Danielle sank into an overstuffed armchair and put her cup on the table beside her. Actually, she'd already known Lee was well. Doctor Bonet had told her. She'd telephoned him after she'd checked into a tiny hotel in Nice.

Sighing deeply, she lay her head back and closed her eyes. Lee had left her so quickly that what had come after was little more than a blur. She remembered going slowly to her room, pulling down her luggage, and tossing her clothing helter-skelter into it. Then she'd hopped into the rental car and ended up in Nice.

It hadn't been too hard to find a relatively inexpensive hotel. The summer season had just about been over, and tourists had been deserting the city in droves. It would fill again in winter, but then accommodation had been readily available.

She'd ended up in a pleasant little place with a view of the water, if you stood on your toes and hung your head far enough out of the window. Once settled into her room, she had stared at the telephone, then snatched it up and put through a call to Dr Bonet.

The surgeon had seemed surprised to hear from her. 'Ah, Mademoiselle Nichols. I asked after you, but Monsieur Bradford said you were no longer in his employ.'

In his employ. The words had cut like a knife. Somehow, she had drawn herself together and asked the only question that mattered.

'Did you take the cast off?'

'*Oui*. As expected, *mademoiselle*.'

'And? How is the leg?'

She'd heard the indrawn sigh of Bonet's breath. 'Also as expected.'

'Then—then there's permanent damage?'

'Yes, of course. Did I not say there would be?' Bonet had hesitated. 'However—your friend's recovery seems most remarkable. His legs are stronger than I anticipated.'

Danielle had bowed her head. She'd been relieved, but not really surprised. 'Yes. Lee said they would be.'

The surgeon had snorted. 'A dubious medical diagnosis, *mademoiselle*.' His voice had softened. 'But an interesting one. I suspect Monsieur Bradford has much to thank you for.'

Her eyes had brimmed with tears. 'No,' she'd said softly, 'he has nothing to thank me for. He did it all himself.'

Now, remembering, her eyes glistened again. She had not seen Lee again, nor had she spoken to him or Val. She had, instead, spent her last days in Nice walking slowly along the waterfront, waiting only for her return flight home.

She sighed as she opened her eyes. She had hoped home would be a safe harbour. And it was—most of the time. But there were still moments when everything caught up with her, moments when she could think of nothing but Lee—his smile, his laugh, the way he'd held her in his arms all through that last night.

And then she would remember how it had ended, how the morning so full of promise had been turned to ashes by the look in his eyes when he'd accused her of sleeping with him out of some kind of twisted pity. She'd remember the expression of revulsion she'd seen on his face that moment before the crash, when he'd put her out of the car.

Danielle shook her head. There was no sense in giving way to self-pity, and that was what she seemed to be doing lately. She had gone into Lee's arms with her eyes wide open, and even if the consequences had been more than she'd anticipated, what did it matter? In the end, he would have left her.

She rose slowly, unbuttoning her blouse as she made her way to the bedroom. A warm shower, a hot cup of tea, and then she'd watch the TV until she was glassy-eyed. There were papers in her briefcase, but there was no rush to get to them. Not tonight.

The telephone rang just as she stepped from the shower. Danielle sighed as she shoved her arms into the sleeves of her old flannel robe, then hurried into her bedroom and lifted the receiver.

'Hello, Ginny,' she said.

Her friend laughed softly. 'Are you into mind-reading, or was that just a good guess?'

She smiled as she sat down on the side of the bed. 'I was going to call you,' she said. 'I wanted to apologise for——'

'Hey. If anybody's gonna do any apologising, it's gonna be me.' Ginny paused. 'Are you OK?'

'I'm fine. I was just going to make myself some tea and turn on the magic box.'

The other woman laughed. 'Sounds like an exciting evening. Susan Miller just called me. She says there's a good movie down at the Film Forum. How would you like me to pick you up on my way to her place?'

Danielle sighed. 'I'm OK,' she said gently. 'Really.'

'We could stop for hot fudge sundaes afterwards. Or pizza.'

She smiled. 'It sounds tempting. But I'll pass.'

'Are you sure?'

'Positive. Have a good time. And say hi to Susan for me.'

Ginny's hesitation was almost palpable. 'All right,' she said finally. 'Talk to you tomorrow.'

Danielle smiled as she hung up the phone and got to her feet. She had the feeling she would hear from Ginny again before the night was over. Another call, just before she left to pick up Susan. Even a quick knock at the door, to see if perhaps Danielle had changed her mind about going with them.

She padded barefoot to the kitchen, switching on the lights as she walked through the dark rooms. Ginny had been more than a good friend these past months, she'd been a kind one. Not too many questions—well, not until today, anyway, she thought as she put the kettle on to boil. And always a smile, or a suggestion of something to do to make the time pass more quickly.

She measured tea into the pot. Still, there were times she simply wanted to be alone. And this was one of them, she thought as she turned off the kettle and poured boiling water into the pot. Sometimes it didn't pay to try and fight off the memories crowding in, no matter how they saddened you. Sometimes——

The doorbell chimed. Danielle put down the tea, smiled, and shook her head as she padded into the living-room.

'Ginny,' she said, laughing as she pulled the door open, 'you're so predictable. I knew you would——'

She gasped in shock, her words falling away from her like stones. The man in the doorway stared at her, his expression as dark and unreadable as his eyes.

'Hello, Danielle,' Lee said. He waited, then took a step forward. 'Well?' he said impatiently. 'Aren't you going to ask me in?'

CHAPTER TWELVE

'LEE?' What a stupid thing to say. Of course it was Lee. What was he doing here? What did he want? A dozen questions whirled inside her head, but in the end all she could manage was to step back and motion him inside.

He moved past her, bringing the cold night air with him. She stared after him, then shut the door and leaned back against it. Lee. Lee, here, in St Louis. It was impossible. He was in—he was in Buenos Aires, getting ready for a race. He. . .

Say something, she told herself. For heaven's sake, don't just stand here.

'Would you—would you like some tea?' she asked.

Had she really said that? This man whom she hadn't seen in five months suddenly turned up in her living-room, and here she was, offering him tea as if——

'Something stronger, if you have it.' He turned towards her. 'I've been driving for hours—I need something to take the kinks out of my legs.'

Danielle blinked. Driving? From Buenos Aires? Her eyes went to his legs, and she blinked again. No cane. He had no cane. And he was standing and walking and. . .

She forced her eyes to meet his. 'I have some sherry. Or brandy, if you prefer.'

He nodded wearily. 'Brandy's fine.' He gestured towards the sofa. 'Do you mind if I sit?'

'No. No, of course not.' She hurried ahead of him, pushing aside the little table she'd been trying to refinish, snatching a magazine out of the way, smoothing down the Afghan draped over the back of a wing-chair like a nervous housewife. Stop that, she thought, and she straightened and turned towards him, just in time to see him take the last steps towards the sofa.

Her heart turned over. He was limping. She hadn't seen it at first, she'd been too stunned, but she could see it now. The limp was slight, but it was there. And he looked—he looked terrible. Fatigued. No—exhausted. And thin. And——

His eyes met hers. She felt the quick catch of her breath, and then she turned and walked quickly towards the kitchen.

'Brandy,' she said. 'I'll just be. . .'

In the safety of the other room, Danielle slumped back against the wall and drew a shuddering breath deep into her lungs. Was she dreaming? Had her desperate heart and mind conjured up Lee's image? Maybe—maybe she would awaken in a little while, alone in her bed, with all this an already fading dream.

She swallowed hard. Whatever Lee was—fantasy or reality—he looked as if he badly needed a drink. And so did she, she thought. Her hands trembled as she poured two generous glasses. Then she took a last steadying breath and stepped into the living-room again.

He was sitting on the sofa, his head laid back and his eyes closed. One leg was propped on the coffee-table in front of him.

Danielle cleared her throat. 'Lee?' she said softly. His eyes opened quickly and his head came up. 'I brought your brandy.'

Their fingers brushed as he took the glass from her. A tremor went through her, racing like a jolt of electricity from her hand to her heart. Lee's eyes leaped to hers. Look away, she told herself, look away while you still can.

'I thought you were in Argentina,' she said, sitting down carefully in the chair opposite him.

He nodded. 'I was.'

She waited for him to say something more. She cleared her throat, to break the silence. 'You've had a good season,' she said. 'Firsts in two races, and—and. . .'

Why was he looking at her that way? There was no expression on his face at all, nothing she could read. His eyes were flat, his mouth hard. What did he want? Why was he here?

'You look like hell,' he said.

His voice was as flat as his eyes. She looked at him, her mouth twisting a little before she spoke.

'Thanks,' she said wryly. She glanced down at her old bathrobe and bare feet. Her hand went to her damp hair, then to the front of the robe. Her fingers dug into the fabric as she tugged the lapels together. 'I wasn't expecting company.'

'I meant *you*,' he said, dismissing the robe and all the rest with a wave of his hand. 'You've lost weight. There are circles under your eyes.'

Her chin lifted. 'You're not exactly an advertisement for the "beautiful people" yourself.'

That was a lie. He was. He always would be. But now he looked somehow frayed at the edges—worn out. She ached to go to him, to stroke away the grooves on either side of his mouth, to kiss away the furrows that rose between his eyebrows.

A tight smile angled across his lips. 'I'll drink to that,' he said, tilting the glass to his mouth. He swallowed down half the brandy, and then he swung his leg to the floor. 'How have you been, Danielle?'

She stared at him. 'Did you come all the way from Buenoss Aires to ask after my health?'

Lee laughed. 'At least that hasn't changed,' he said, drinking down the rest of the brandy. 'You still know how to get straight to the point.' He rose and started towards the kitchen. 'Mind if I help myself?'

'I'll do it,' she said, hurrying after him. 'You just sit and. . .'

But he had already reached the kitchen and picked up the bottle. 'I don't need mollycoddling,' he said sharply.

Danielle's mouth tightened as she watched him. The lights were brighter in here; they illuminated his face with cruelty. He looked even worse than she'd thought. There was dark stubble on his cheeks and chin, but under it his skin had a greyish cast.

What in God's name was he doing here?

'What *do* you need, then?' she asked.

Lee stared at her. 'What's that supposed to mean?'

She swallowed. 'Just what I said. You—you don't look very well. And now you—you turn up in my living-room and. . .' She inhaled sharply. 'Are you ill? Are your legs——?'

He put the brandy bottle down on the counter. 'Do you care?'

His voice was cold. The sound of it sent a chill along her flesh. No, she wanted to say, just as coldly, no, I don't care a damn. If you've come here for my help, you can go straight to hell.

Her shoulders sagged. It was a nice, satisfying thought—but it was a lie. Lee despised her. He'd made that clear enough. Still, if he was hurting, if he needed her. . .

No. She loved him, but she couldn't help him. Not this time. The price was too high.

She turned away from him. 'If you've finished your brandy,' she said, 'I think you'd better——'

Lee covered the distance between them quickly, and his hands closed on her shoulders.

'Dammit!' He spun her towards him and glared down at her, his eyes dark and dangerous. 'I spent eight and a half hours on a plane to Miami, another God knows how many in a rental car——'

'Is that supposed to be my fault?' she said, lifting her eyes to his. Yes, she thought, get angry with him. Remember how he treated you that last day. It's better than—than. . .

'Aren't you even going to ask me why I'm here?'

She took a breath. 'All right,' she said quietly. 'Why *are* you here?'

'I was going to fly,' he said, glowering at her, ignoring the question he'd demanded she ask. 'I'd have been here hours ago if I had, and my damned legs wouldn't be reminding me that they're a hundred years old, even if the rest of me isn't.'

'Then why didn't you?' she said. 'And stop trying to make it sound as if it's my fault you left Argentina, my fault you drove all that rotten distance, my fault you——'

'Flying was too quick,' he said angrily, his eyes sweeping across her face. 'I wanted to get here, but—but not until—not until. . .' He fell silent and stared at her while the seconds ticked away, and then his hands dropped to his sides. 'God,' he said softly, 'I went over this a dozen times the past thousand miles. I had it all planned—what I was going to say, how I was going to say it. . .' He drew in his breath. 'That's why I drove. I needed the time to work things out. But—but. . .'

Danielle stared at him. 'To work what things out? You're not making any sense at all.'

Lee nodded. 'Yeah. I know. I. . .' He paused. 'Listen,' he said, 'maybe I'd—maybe I'd better leave. I—I shouldn't have walked in on you this way.'

'No!' Her cry of desperation startled her as much as him. It wasn't what she'd meant to say; she'd meant to tell him that leaving was a good idea. Their eyes met, and Danielle swallowed drily. 'I mean, you—you've had a long trip. You might as well. . .' Her voice trembled, then broke. 'Don't go,' she whispered. 'Stay for a little while. Just for a—for a. . .'

She turned away quickly and put her hands to her face. Oh, God, where was her pride? She'd been so determined to remain in control, not to let him glimpse the pain in her heart.

'Why should I?' Lee's hands bit into her shoulders. 'You couldn't wait to get rid of me the last time we were together.'

'That's not true. It was you who——'

He swung her towards him. 'I want answers,' he said sharply. 'And I want them now.'

Danielle's chin rose. 'You can't always get what you want, Lee. Maybe it's time you learned that.'

His eyes flashed a warning. 'Why did you let me make love to you that night?'

Danielle stared at him. 'I don't believe it,' she said. 'Is that what this is all about? Did you come all this distance to start that nonsense again?'

'I asked you a question, dammit. And I want an answer.'

'Well, you're not going to get one. Go away, Lee. Go back to Buenos Aires and——'

'A few minutes ago, you begged me to stay.'

'I didn't beg,' she said quickly. But she had, and they both knew it. Danielle felt her courage leak away like air from a balloon. Her gaze slipped from his and she looked down at the floor. 'Do us both a favour,' she said quietly. 'Just—just go away.'

'Look at me,' Lee demanded.

'No. For God's sake, haven't you humiliated me enough? Must you——?'

His hand cupped her face. 'I said look at me, Danielle.'

The pressure of his fingers was impossible to withstand. Her head came up slowly, but not her eyes.

Whatever game he was playing now was the cruellest one of all. She wouldn't—she wouldn't. . .

'Danielle.' His voice was soft, as was the touch of his hand as he wiped away the tears that were sliding down her cheeks. 'Danielle, sweetheart, look at me. Please.'

Slowly, slowly, she raised her eyes to his. Her heartbeat quickened. He was smiling, a sweet smile as intimate as any he'd given her on that far-away night.

'Lee?'

Her whisper hung in the air, a thousand questions dancing within it, and he answered them all by kissing her.

Danielle trembled. This was crazy. What was going on here? A man whose life was excitement and glamour wouldn't walk away from a Grand Prix, fly across a continent, then drive who knew how many miles just so he could kiss a woman he'd taken to his bed one long-ago night during a hot summer in Provence.

Her eyes opened slowly as he took his mouth from hers. His hands clasped her face and he smiled again.

'You still haven't answered my question,' he said softly. 'Tell me why you made love with me in Provence.'

'That's—that's a stupid question. I don't have to answer——'

Lee's expression became serious. 'Yes, you do.'

'I don't. And I won't.'

She struggled wildly as he bent towards her. His mouth closed over hers and he kissed her slowly, deeply. No, she told herself, no, don't kiss him back.

But it was too late. She was melting against him, losing herself in his kiss. Lee's hands slid to her shoulders, then to her back. His arms went around her, gathering her tightly to him. Danielle lifted her arms and twined them around his neck. It had been so long since she'd held him, so long since she'd felt the silken stroke of his mouth on hers.

A smothered sound caught in her throat, part-sob, part-laugh. Maybe this *was* a dream. Maybe she really was tucked into her own bed, imagining everything.

'Danielle.' Her eyes opened slowly as Lee cupped her shoulders and put her from him. He was watching her, a funny little smile on his face. 'It's true, isn't it?'

'What's true?' she said. But she knew. She knew.

'You're in love with me.'

Danielle's mouth trembled. 'I'm not.'

He laughed softly, triumphantly. 'You are. You have been, all along. That's the reason you came into my arms that night.'

She shook her head. 'No. I don't know why you'd think such a ridiculous thing.'

His hands moved to clasp her face again. 'I can give you one very good reason,' he said. 'Because I'm in love with you.'

The world stood still. She was afraid to move, afraid to breathe—surely, if she did, this magic moment would vanish. But Lee's breath was warm on her cheek, his fingers gentle as they traced the curve of her mouth, and suddenly a wild elation filled her.

'I think I should warn you,' she said, her voice shaking just a little, 'that if you're a dream, Lee Bradford, I'm going to be very angry when I wake up.'

Lee laughed. 'If I'm a dream,' he said, dropping light kisses along the curve of her cheek, 'I'm the first I ever heard of whose legs feel as if they might fall off any minute.'

'Oh, Lee!' Danielle clasped his hand and tugged him after her to the sofa. 'Your poor legs.'

He sank down on the sofa and pulled her into his lap. 'Never mind my legs,' he said. His eyes grew dark. 'Where I come from, a woman's supposed to make an appropriate response when a man says he loves her.'

Danielle smiled. 'I love you,' she said, and then she

threw back her head. 'I love you,' she repeated, 'I love——'

Lee pulled her to him and silenced her with a kiss. When it ended, he scowled at her.

'Why didn't you tell me?' he demanded. 'That night, the next morning——'

'Why didn't you tell *me*? Where I come from, a man says those words first.'

'But I did tell you. Hell, I'd spent the night telling you I loved you.' His mouth narrowed. 'I was sure you loved me, too. But the next morning, when I asked you. . .'

Danielle stared at him. 'Asked me what?'

'Don't you remember? I asked you to admit the truth.'

The breath rushed from her lungs. Tell me, he'd said, give me the satisfaction of hearing you say it. And she'd misunderstood, she'd thought—she'd thought. . .

Danielle shook her head. 'I didn't understand. I—I thought you were boasting.'

Lee's eyebrows rose. 'Well, that, too. It had been a night to boast about, hadn't it?' He smiled and drew her closer. 'Danielle,' he said, his smile fading, 'what went wrong that morning? Why did you let me think you'd made love to me out of some misguided sense of compassion?'

She sighed. 'I was a fool,' she said softly. 'I thought you felt grateful to me.'

'Of course I was grateful. You brought me back to life.' He kissed her gently. 'Loving you was the reason I'd worked so damned hard to get well.'

She ran her tongue over her lips. 'And—and then I heard you on the phone with Val. You made a date with her. . .'

Lee sighed. 'Val called because Wexler had told her my cast was coming off that day. He wanted some information from me, and she offered to collect it. I guess she'd decided it wouldn't hurt to see if I was going to be myself again or not. She said she would take a taxi to the cottage—but I didn't want anyone or anything to intrude on us. The only way I could get rid of her was by agreeing to meet her. I suppose it was stupid not to tell you—but I knew how uncomfortable she made you feel.'

'It was because I knew—I knew the two of you had been lovers,' Danielle said softly.

Lee shook his head. 'We were never lovers. Val made it obvious that she wanted to sleep with me,' he said, his gaze steady on hers. 'She'd already worked her way through the director and the second male lead. But I wasn't interested. She collects men instead of autographs, and I had my fill of that kind of thing a long time ago.'

Danielle's eyes searched his. 'And—and you'd already phoned for a taxi. You'd planned on leaving me behind when you went to Nice.'

He nodded. 'Yes. The cast was coming off—that was going to be my moment of truth, and I had to face it alone.'

'Alone? Why did you have to do it alone?'

'For the same reason I didn't tell you I loved you. I was afraid I might be crippled. And I didn't want to tie you to half a man.'

Danielle's eyes glistened with unshed tears. 'You're a fool, Lee Bradford,' she whispered. 'Don't you know I'd love you and want you no matter what?'

He smiled and stroked the curls back from her temples. 'I've dreamed about you these last months,' he said. 'I hated you and loved you at the same time, and it was killing me. How could she have come to me that night without loving me? I kept thinking. How could she have seen me through those awful weeks without caring?'

'Oh, Lee. I did care. And I loved you.'

'Hush,' he whispered, kissing her tenderly. 'I know that now.' He sighed. 'I wish I could say it came through some stroke of brilliance, darling. But the truth is that I was lying awake the other night, thinking about you, remembering how it had been between us—and suddenly I remembered what had happened just before the accident, when you and I were together.'

Danielle's smile dimmed. 'How you hated me that evening,' she said softly. 'It broke my heart when I saw the way you looked at me, the disgust in your eyes—and then, that last morning at the cottage, I saw that same terrible expression on your face. No,' she said quickly, putting her hand over his mouth, 'don't try to explain. Whatever it was, is over. I don't want to know about it.'

Lee kissed her palm, then caught her hand in his. 'But you're wrong, my love. I never hated you, not for a second. Yes, you saw disgust in my face the night of the crash—disgust for myself. I was going to seduce you—it was why I'd brought you to the inn.' He smiled at her. 'But then I kissed you, and I couldn't take you inside, even though I knew you would go with me.'

'I would have,' she said. 'I wanted you so, Lee. I was in love with you already, even though I hadn't admitted it to myself.'

'You came into my arms as if—as if you'd waited all your life for me to find you. You kissed me as if you wanted to belong to me forever.'

Danielle nodded. 'Yes. I remember.'

'It was the same the night we made love at the cottage. And when I realised that, I saw the truth. I knew I'd made a terrible mistake, that you'd loved me and wanted me *before* I'd been hurt, *before* you'd become my angel of mercy.' He smiled into her eyes. 'And I knew that pity wasn't what had brought you into my arms.'

Danielle smiled back at him. 'I've always loved you,'

she said softly. 'Somehow, I think I must have loved you all my life.'

Lee's arms tightened around her. 'I said such awful things to you that last day. I didn't mean any of them. It was just that my heart was broken.'

She looped her arms around his neck and pressed her forehead to his. 'I said some foolish things, too. Eddie—Eddie had nothing to do with why I wanted to help you recover, Lee. I did it because I loved you.'

He smiled. 'I'll forgive you if you'll forgive me. How does that sound?'

Danielle laughed softly. 'I don't know,' she said, tilting her head back and looking at him. 'You might have to convince me.'

Lee grinned. 'Maybe we can work something out.' He shifted her in his arms and got to his feet. 'Which way's the bedroom? We can start our negotiating in there.'

'That way,' she said. 'But I warn you, I drive a hard bargain.'

'You won't get anywhere until you agree to the ground rules,' Lee warned as he carried her through the living-room. 'First, you have to promise to stick with me even though I've decided to give up racing.'

Her heart soared. 'Give it up? Oh, Lee, I'm so glad. I mean, I know you love racing. But I've worried so these past months. . .'

He paused beside her bed and gave her a deep, lingering kiss. 'The second part of the bargain's tougher,' he whispered. 'You have to agree to marry me.'

Her eyes glistened. 'I don't know,' she said with a toss of her head. 'That might take some convincing.'

Lee smiled as he lowered her to the bed. 'How much?'

Danielle caught his face between her hands and brought his mouth to hers. 'Hours' worth,' she murmured. 'Until dawn, at least.'

He laughed softly as he came down beside her. 'I was hoping you'd say that.'

Danielle sighed as Lee's arms closed around her. After a lifetime of searching, the quest was ended.

She had found Lee—and she had found love.

HARLEQUIN

Romance®

This December, travel to Northport, Massachusetts, with Harlequin Romance FIRST CLASS title #3164, A TOUCH OF FORGIVENESS by Emma Goldrick

FIRST CLASS

Folks in Northport called Kitty the meanest woman in town, but she couldn't forget how they had duped her brother and exploited her family's land. It was hard to be mean, though, when Joel Carmody was around—his calm, good humor made Kitty feel like a new woman. Nevertheless, a Carmody was a Carmody, and the name meant money and power to the townspeople.... Could Kitty really trust Joel, or was he like all the rest?

If you missed September title #3149, ROSES HAVE THORNS (England), October title #3155, TRAPPED (England) or November title #3159, AN ANSWER FROM THE HEART (England) and would like to order any of them, send your name, address, zip or postal code, along with a check or money order for $2.99 plus 75¢ postage and handling ($1.00 in Canada) for each book ordered, payable to Harlequin Reader Service to:

In the U.S.
3010 Walden Avenue
P.O. Box 1325
Buffalo, NY 14269-1325

In Canada
P.O. Box 609
Fort Erie, Ontario
L2A 5X3

Please specify book title(s) with your order.
Canadian residents add applicable federal and provincial taxes.

JT-B12R

Bring back heartwarming memories of Christmas past with HISTORICAL CHRISTMAS STORIES 1991, a collection of romantic stories by three popular authors. The perfect Christmas gift!

Don't miss these heartwarming stories, available in November wherever Harlequin books are sold:

CHRISTMAS YET TO COME
by Linda Trent
A SEASON OF JOY
by Caryn Cameron
FORTUNE'S GIFT
by DeLoras Scott

Best Wishes and Season's Greetings from Harlequin!

XM-91

HARLEQUIN

Romance®

A Christmas tradition...

Imagine spending Christmas in New Orleans with a blind stranger and his aged guide dog—when you're supposed to be there on your honeymoon!
#3163 Every Kind of Heaven
by Bethany Campbell

Imagine spending Christmas with a man you once "married"—in a mock ceremony at the age of eight!
#3166 The Forgetful Bride
by Debbie Macomber

Available in December 1991, wherever Harlequin books are sold.

RXM

"INDULGE A LITTLE" SWEEPSTAKES

HERE'S HOW THE SWEEPSTAKES WORKS

NO PURCHASE NECESSARY

To enter each drawing, complete the appropriate Official Entry Form or a 3" by 5" index card by hand-printing your name, address and phone number and the trip destination that the entry is being submitted for (i.e., Walt Disney World Vacation Drawing, etc.) and mailing it to: Indulge '91 Subscribers-Only Sweepstakes, P.O. Box 1397, Buffalo, New York 14269-1397.

No responsibility is assumed for lost, late or misdirected mail. Entries must be sent separately with first class postage affixed, and be received by: 9/30/91 for the Walt Disney World Vacation Drawing, 10/31/91 for the Alaskan Cruise Drawing and 11/30/91 for the Hawaiian Vacation Drawing. Sweepstakes is open to residents of the U.S. and Canada, 21 years of age or older as of 11/7/91.

For complete rules, send a self-addressed, stamped (WA residents need not affix return postage) envelope to: Indulge '91 Subscribers-Only Sweepstakes Rules, P.O. Box 4005, Blair, NE 68009.

© 1991 HARLEQUIN ENTERPRISES LTD. DIR-RL

"INDULGE A LITTLE" SWEEPSTAKES

HERE'S HOW THE SWEEPSTAKES WORKS

NO PURCHASE NECESSARY

To enter each drawing, complete the appropriate Official Entry Form or a 3" by 5" index card by hand-printing your name, address and phone number and the trip destination that the entry is being submitted for (i.e., Walt Disney World Vacation Drawing, etc.) and mailing it to: Indulge '91 Subscribers-Only Sweepstakes, P.O. Box 1397, Buffalo, New York 14269-1397.

No responsibility is assumed for lost, late or misdirected mail. Entries must be sent separately with first class postage affixed, and be received by: 9/30/91 for the Walt Disney World Vacation Drawing, 10/31/91 for the Alaskan Cruise Drawing and 11/30/91 for the Hawaiian Vacation Drawing. Sweepstakes is open to residents of the U.S. and Canada, 21 years of age or older as of 11/7/91.

For complete rules, send a self-addressed, stamped (WA residents need not affix return postage) envelope to: Indulge '91 Subscribers-Only Sweepstakes Rules, P.O. Box 4005, Blair, NE 68009.

© 1991 HARLEQUIN ENTERPRISES LTD. DIR-RL

INDULGE A LITTLE—WIN A LOT!

Summer of '91 Subscribers-Only Sweepstakes

OFFICIAL ENTRY FORM

This entry must be received by: Oct. 31, 1991
This month's winner will be notified by: Nov. 7, 1991
Trip must be taken between: May 27, 1992—Sept. 9, 1992
(depending on sailing schedule)

YES, I want to win the Alaska Cruise vacation for two. I understand the prize includes round-trip airfare, one-week cruise including private cabin, all meals and pocket money as revealed on the "wallet" scratch-off card.

Name ____________

Address ____________ Apt. ______

City ____________

State/Prov. ______ Zip/Postal Code ______

Daytime phone number ____________
(Area Code)

Return entries with invoice in envelope provided. Each book in this shipment has two entry coupons—and the more coupons you enter, the better your chances of winning!

© 1991 HARLEQUIN ENTERPRISES LTD. 2N-CPS

INDULGE A LITTLE—WIN A LOT!

Summer of '91 Subscribers-Only Sweepstakes

OFFICIAL ENTRY FORM

This entry must be received by: Oct. 31, 1991
This month's winner will be notified by: Nov. 7, 1991
Trip must be taken between: May 27, 1992—Sept. 9, 1992
(depending on sailing schedule)

YES, I want to win the Alaska Cruise vacation for two. I understand the prize includes round-trip airfare, one-week cruise including private cabin, all meals and pocket money as revealed on the "wallet" scratch-off card.

Name ____________

Address ____________ Apt. ______

City ____________

State/Prov. ______ Zip/Postal Code ______

Daytime phone number ____________
(Area Code)

Return entries with invoice in envelope provided. Each book in this shipment has two entry coupons—and the more coupons you enter, the better your chances of winning!

© 1991 HARLEQUIN ENTERPRISES LTD. 2N-CPS